FAR OUT
FOLKTALES

STONE ARCH BOOKS
a capstone imprint

INTRODUCING...

JOHNNY SLIMESEED

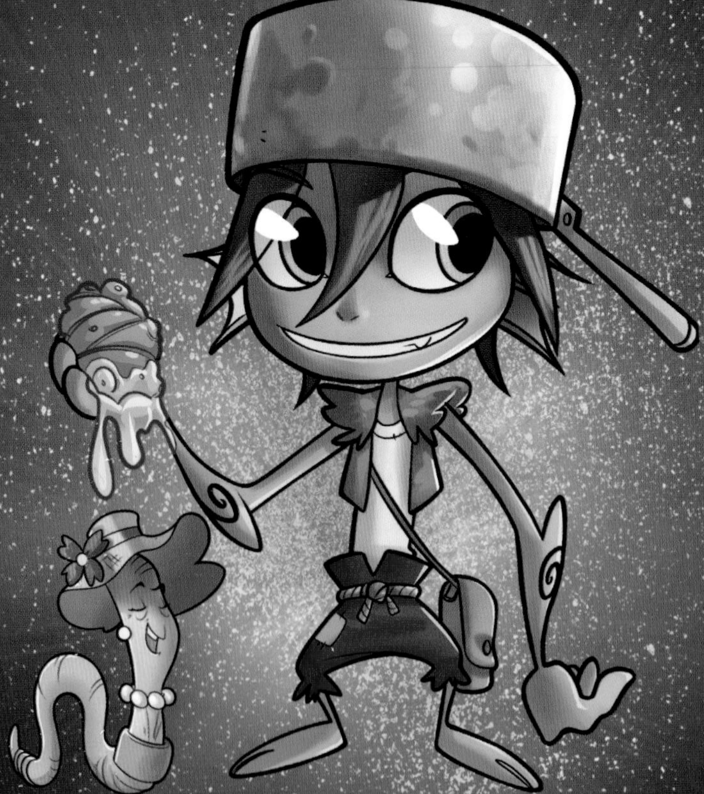

SLEEKA THE WORM

JOHNNY'S CLASSMATES

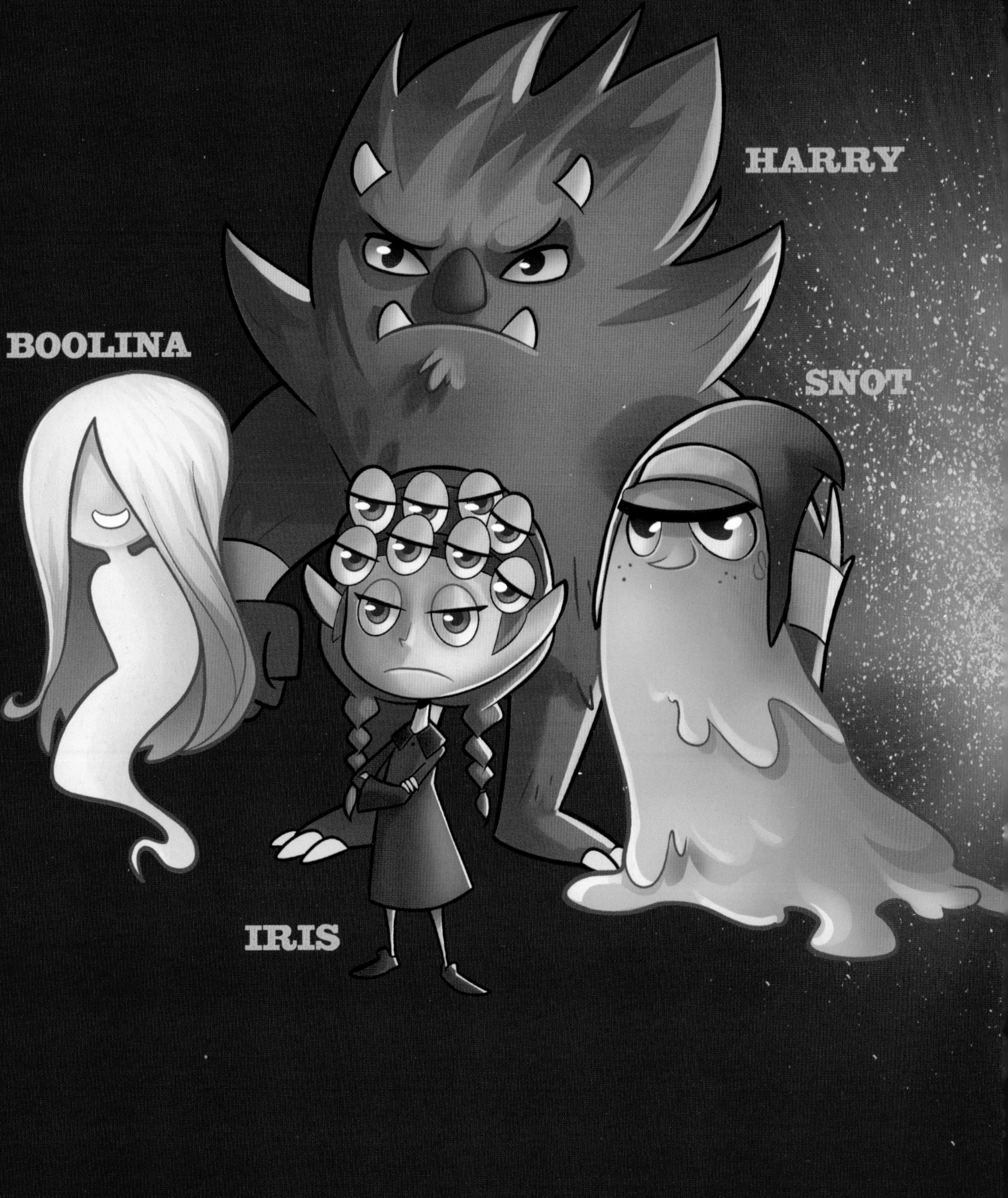
HARRY
BOOLINA
SNOT
IRIS

IN...

Far Out Folktales is published by
Stone Arch Books
A Capstone Imprint
1710 Roe Crest Drive
North Mankato, Minnesota 56003
www.mycapstone.com

Cataloging-in-Publication Data is
available at the Library of Congress
website.
ISBN 978-1-4965-7843-3 (hardcover)
ISBN 978-1-4965-8008-5 (paperback)
ISBN 978-1-4965-7848-8 (eBook PDF)

Summary: Johnny Slimeseed isn't like the
other monsters in Nightmare. The gentle
swamp creature hates scaring human
kids and wishes his fellow ghouls would
find another hobby. So he comes up
with a plan—fill the land with oozy slime
trees! If he can plant enough, monsters
won't frighten anyone because they'll be
too busy having fun in the sludge. Can
Johnny achieve his freaky forest dream?

Designed by Brann Garvey
Edited by Abby Huff
Lettered by Jaymes Reed

Printed and bound in China.
966

FAR OUT FOLKTALES

JOHNNY SLIMESEED and the FREAKY FOREST

A GRAPHIC NOVEL

by **Stephanie True Peters**

illustrated by **Berenice Muñiz**

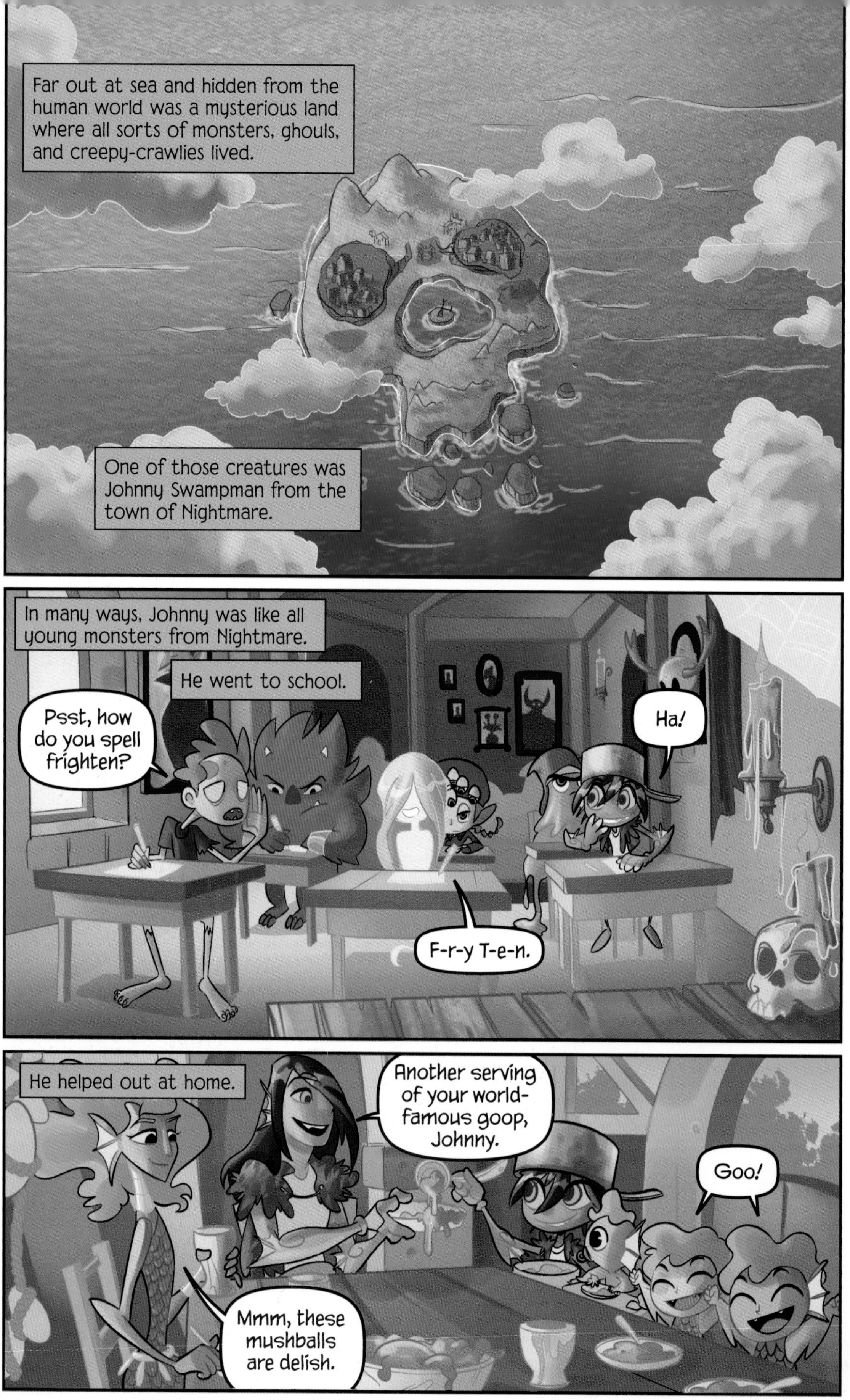
Far out at sea and hidden from the human world was a mysterious land where all sorts of monsters, ghouls, and creepy-crawlies lived.
One of those creatures was Johnny Swampman from the town of Nightmare.
In many ways, Johnny was like all young monsters from Nightmare.
He went to school.
Psst, how do you spell frighten?
Ha!
F-r-y T-e-n.
He helped out at home.
Another serving of your world-famous goop, Johnny.
Goo!
Mmm, these mushballs are delish.

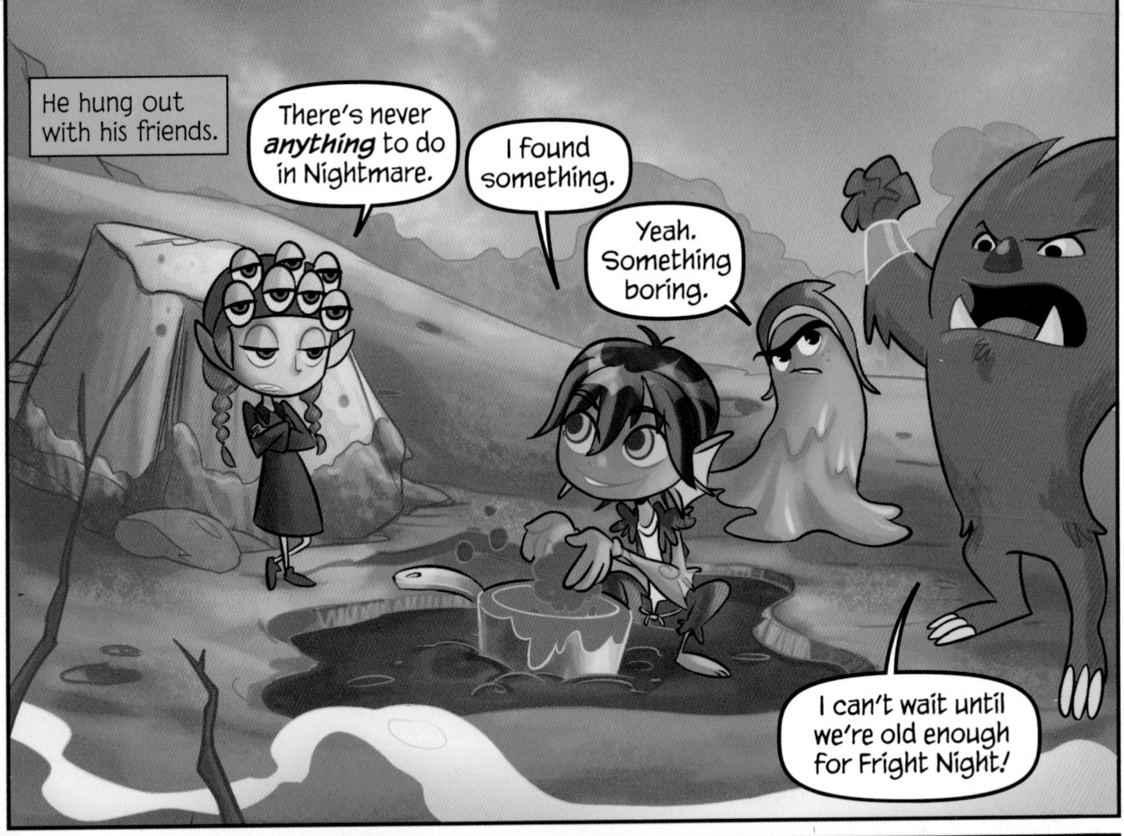
He hung out with his friends.
There's never *anything* to do in Nightmare.
I found something.
Yeah. Something boring.
I can't wait until we're old enough for Fright Night!

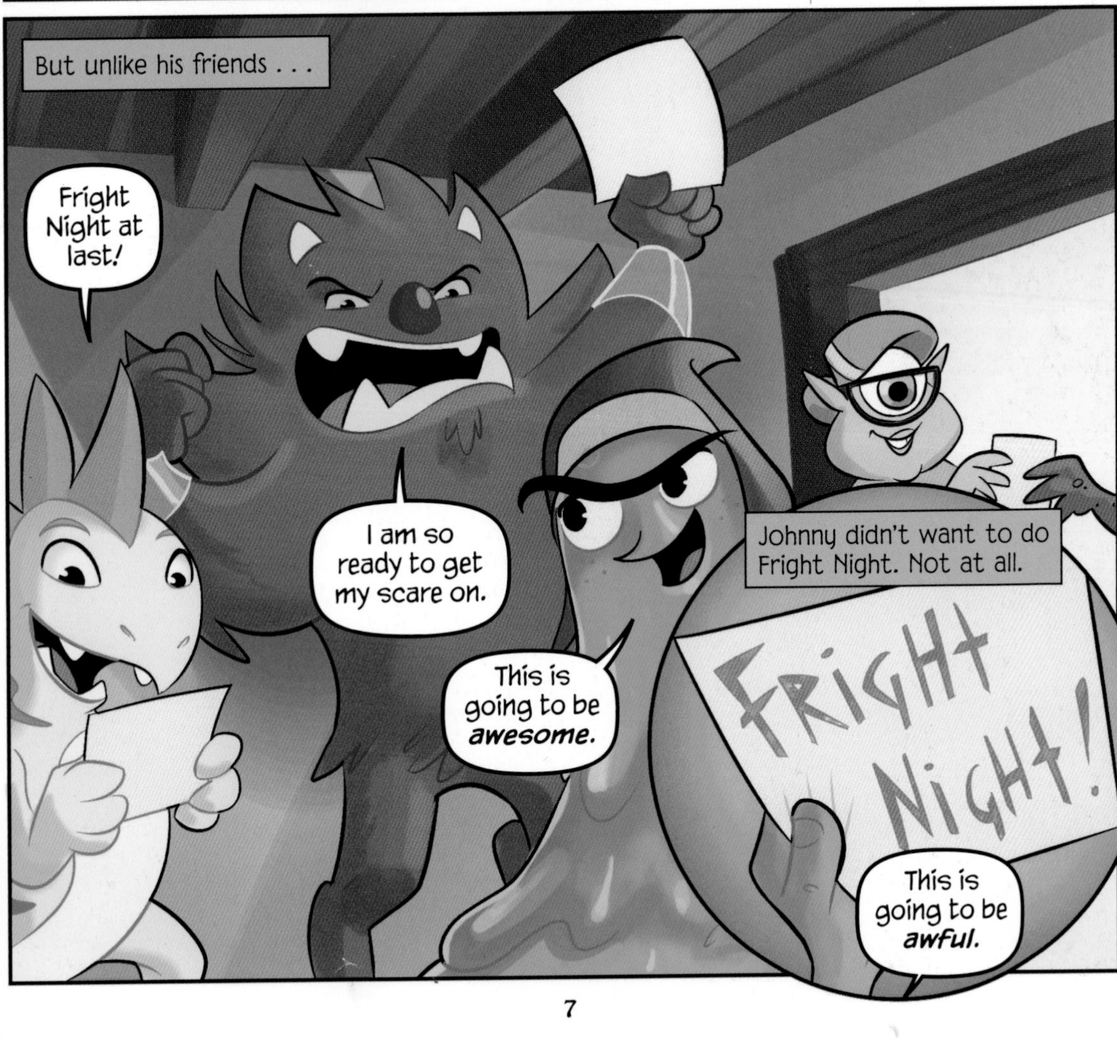
But unlike his friends . . .
Fright Night at last!
I am so ready to get my scare on.
This is going to be *awesome*.
Johnny didn't want to do Fright Night. Not at all.
FRIGHT NIGHT!
This is going to be *awful*.

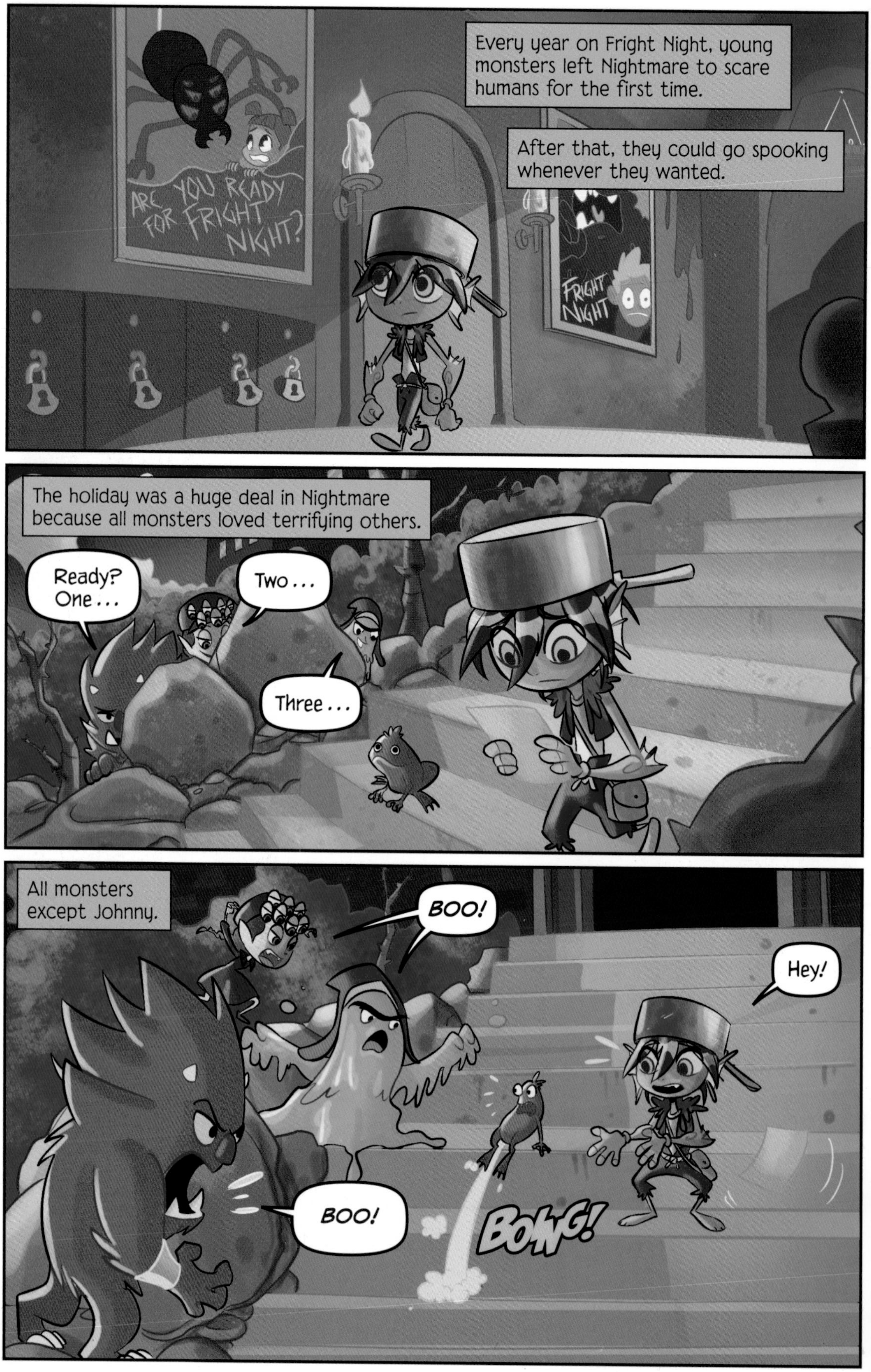
ARE YOU READY FOR FRIGHT NIGHT?
Every year on Fright Night, young monsters left Nightmare to scare humans for the first time.
After that, they could go spooking whenever they wanted.
FRIGHT NIGHT
The holiday was a huge deal in Nightmare because all monsters loved terrifying others.
Ready? One...
Two...
Three...
All monsters except Johnny.
BOO!
Hey!
BOO!
BOING!

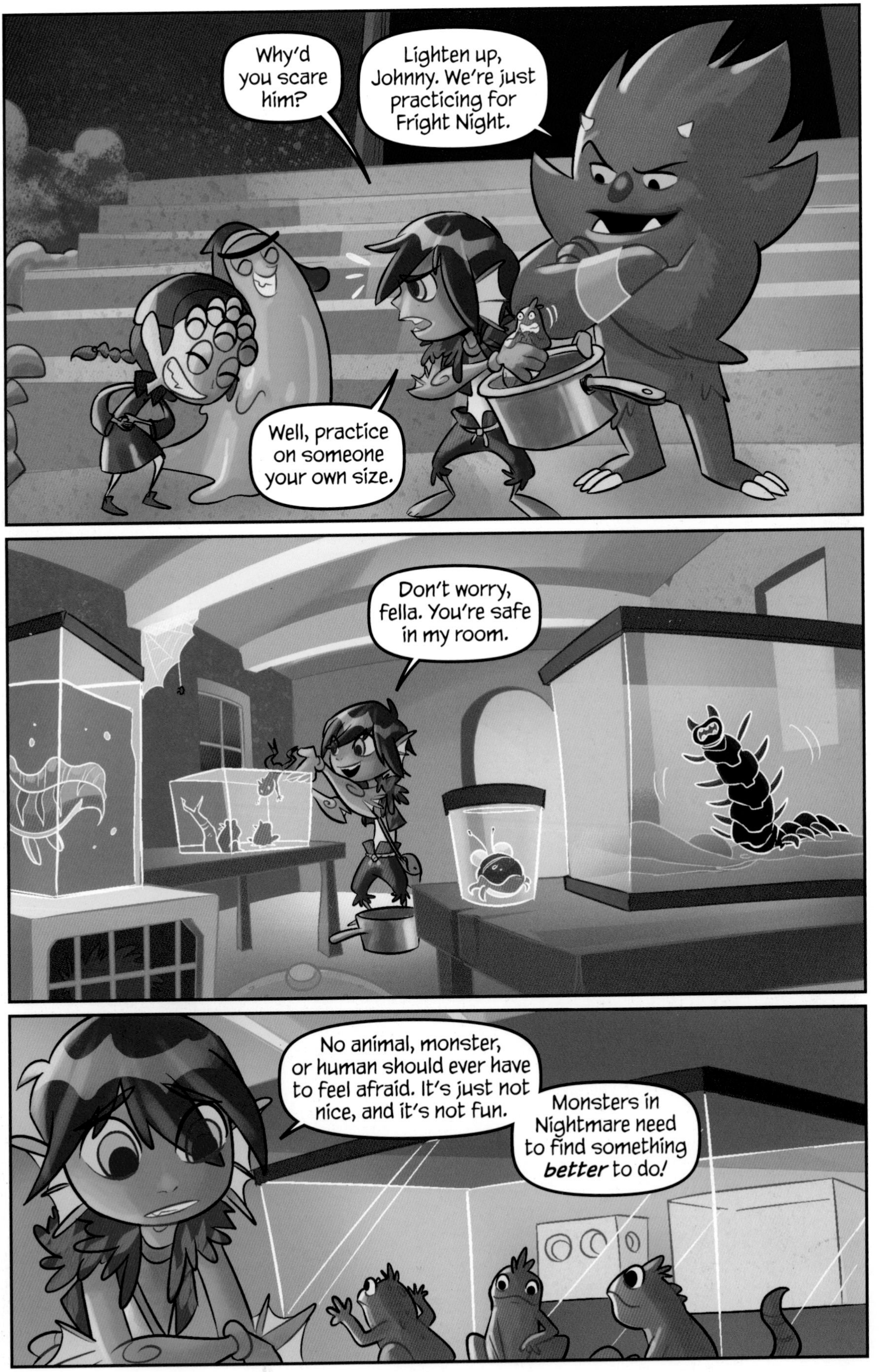
Why'd you scare him?
Lighten up, Johnny. We're just practicing for Fright Night.
Well, practice on someone your own size.
Don't worry, fella. You're safe in my room.
No animal, monster, or human should ever have to feel afraid. It's just not nice, and it's not fun.
Monsters in Nightmare need to find something **better** to do!

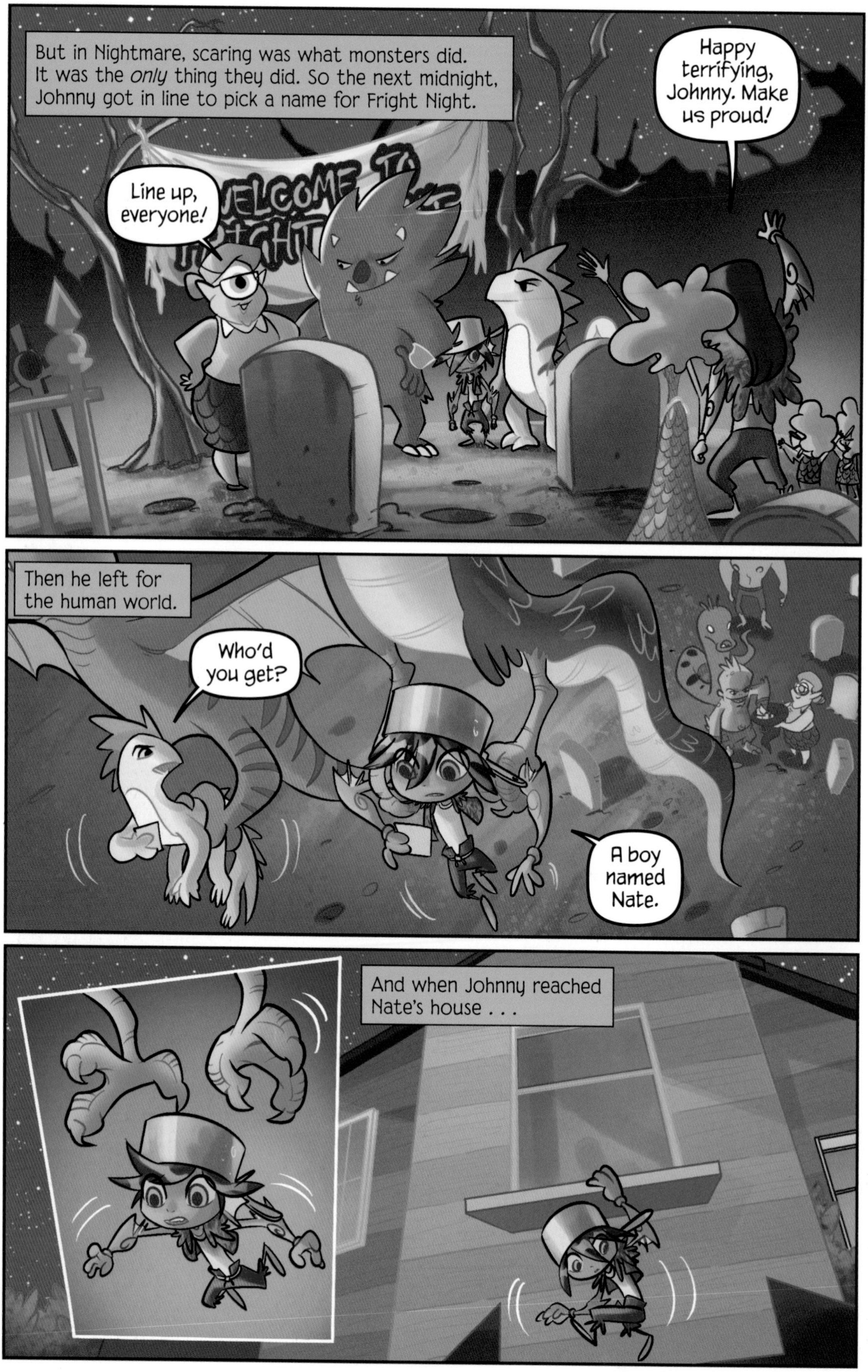
But in Nightmare, scaring was what monsters did. It was the *only* thing they did. So the next midnight, Johnny got in line to pick a name for Fright Night.
Happy terrifying, Johnny. Make us proud!
Line up, everyone!
Then he left for the human world.
Who'd you get?
A boy named Nate.
And when Johnny reached Nate's house . . .

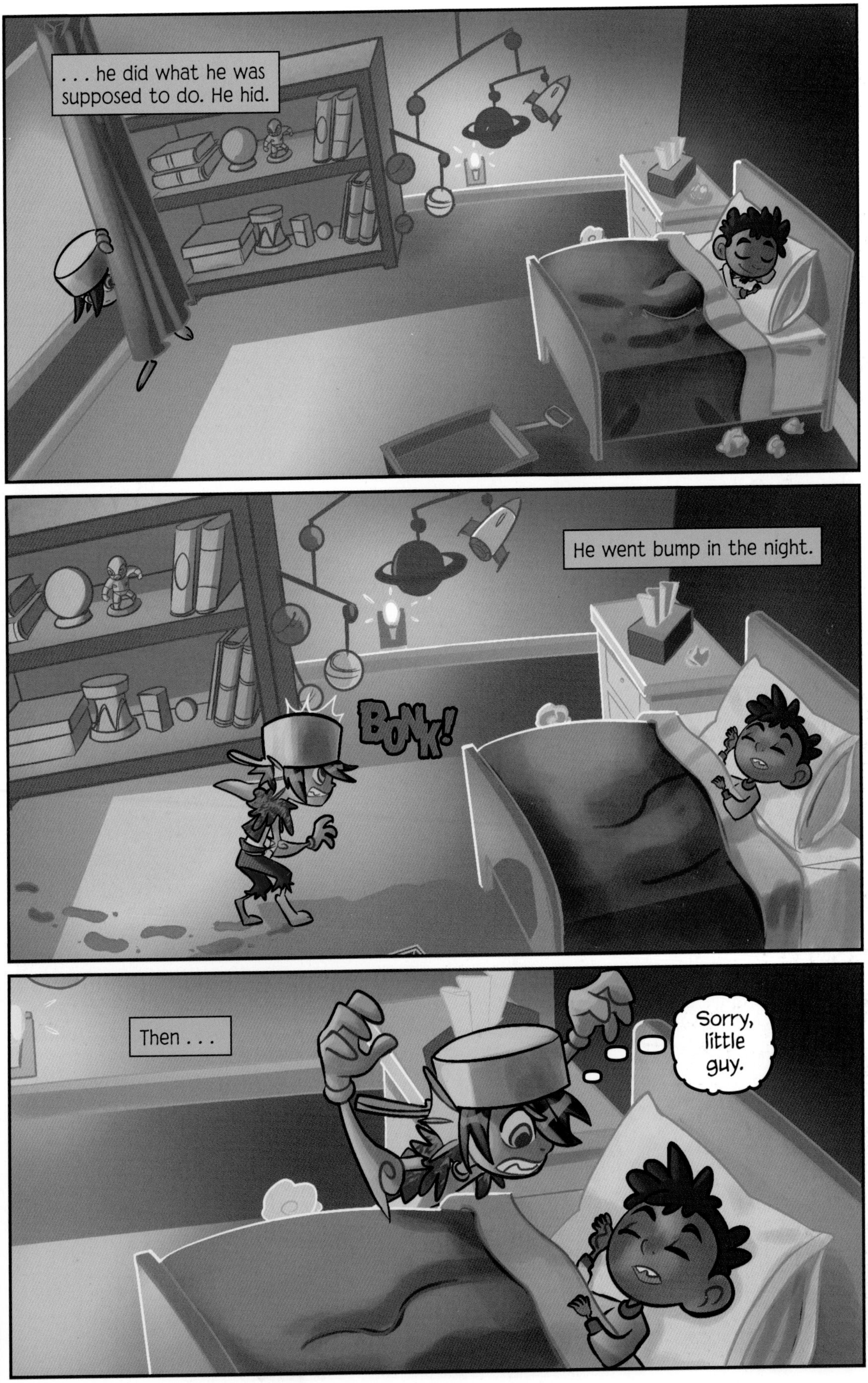
. . . he did what he was supposed to do. He hid.
He went bump in the night.
BONK!
Then . . .
Sorry, little guy.

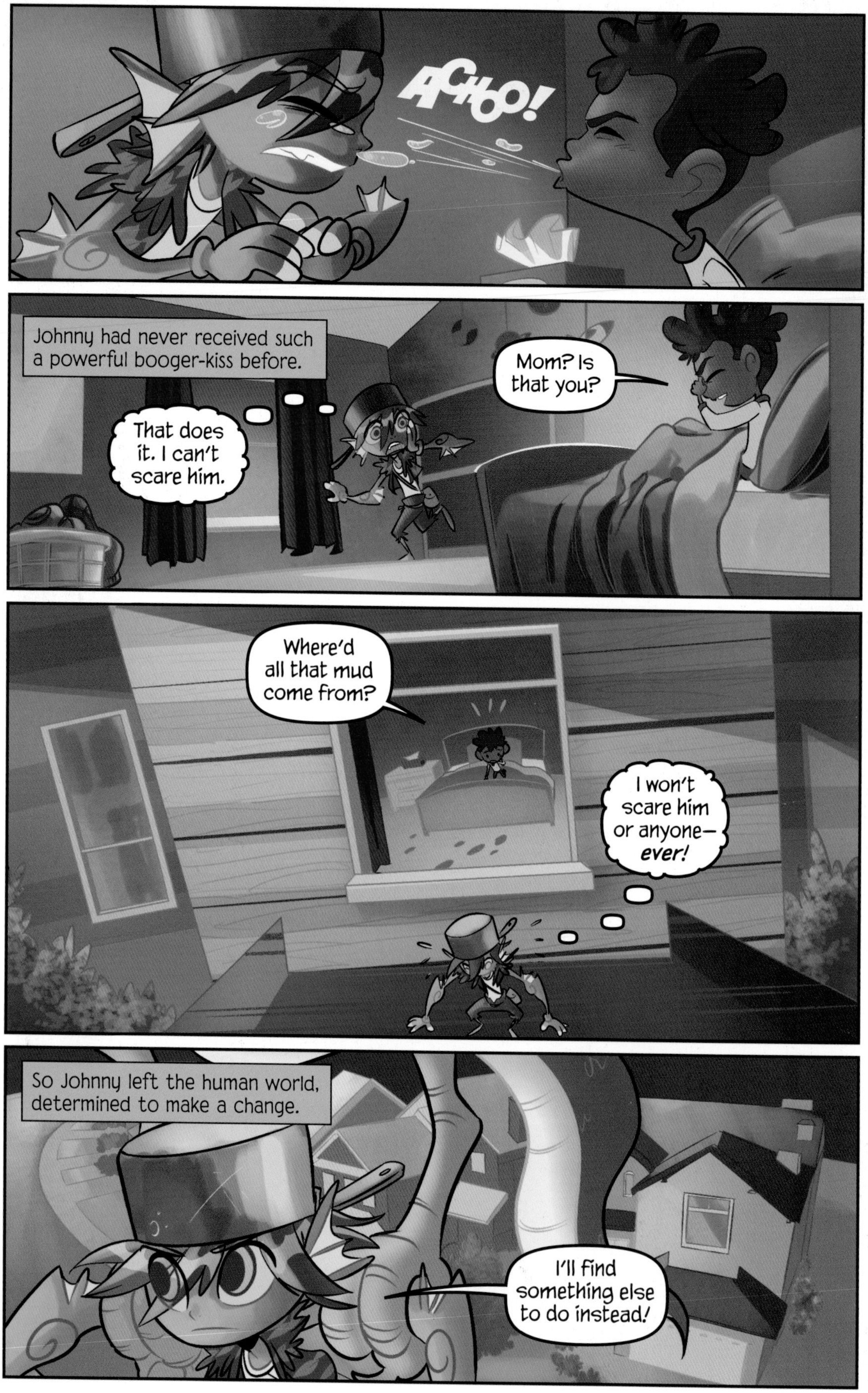
ACHOO!
Johnny had never received such a powerful booger-kiss before.
Mom? Is that you?
That does it. I can't scare him.
Where'd all that mud come from?
I won't scare him or anyone—*ever!*
So Johnny left the human world, determined to make a change.
I'll find something else to do instead!

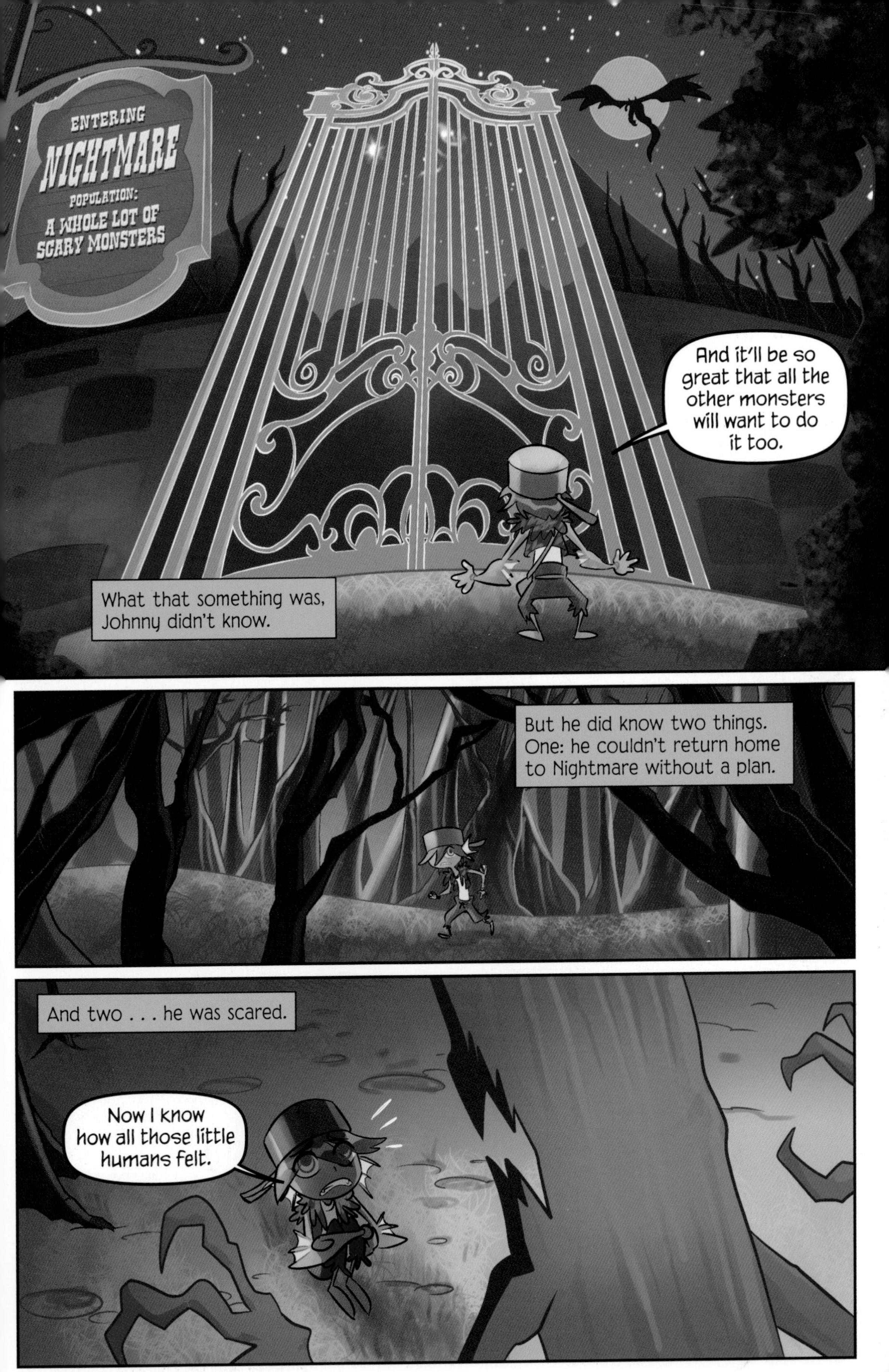
ENTERING NIGHTMARE POPULATION: A WHOLE LOT OF SCARY MONSTERS
And it'll be so great that all the other monsters will want to do it too.
What that something was, Johnny didn't know.
But he did know two things. One: he couldn't return home to Nightmare without a plan.
And two . . . he was scared.
Now I know how all those little humans felt.

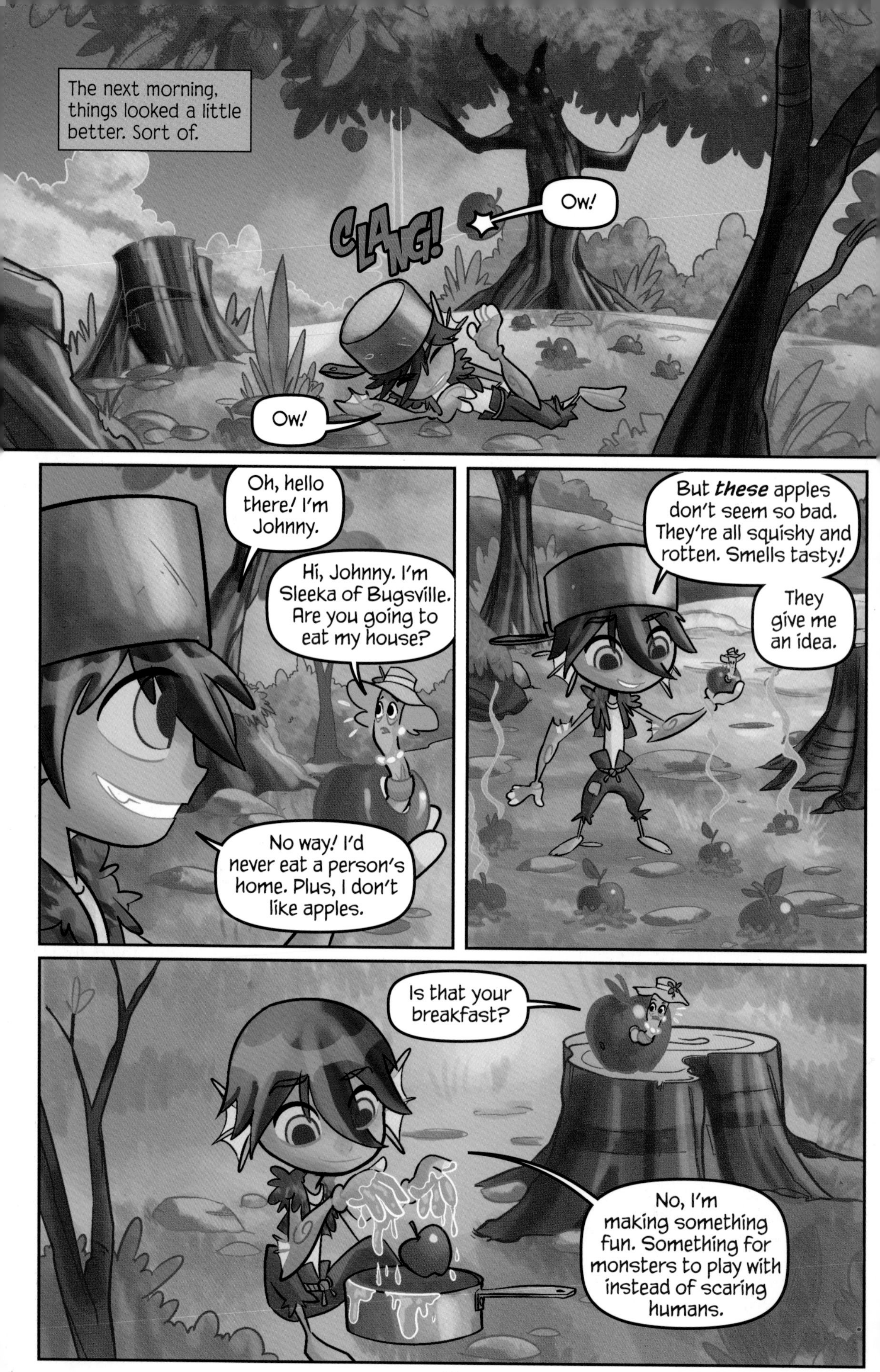
The next morning, things looked a little better. Sort of.
CLANG!
Ow!
Ow!
Oh, hello there! I'm Johnny.
Hi, Johnny. I'm Sleeka of Bugsville. Are you going to eat my house?
No way! I'd never eat a person's home. Plus, I don't like apples.
But *these* apples don't seem so bad. They're all squishy and rotten. Smells tasty!
They give me an idea.
Is that your breakfast?
No, I'm making something fun. Something for monsters to play with instead of scaring humans.

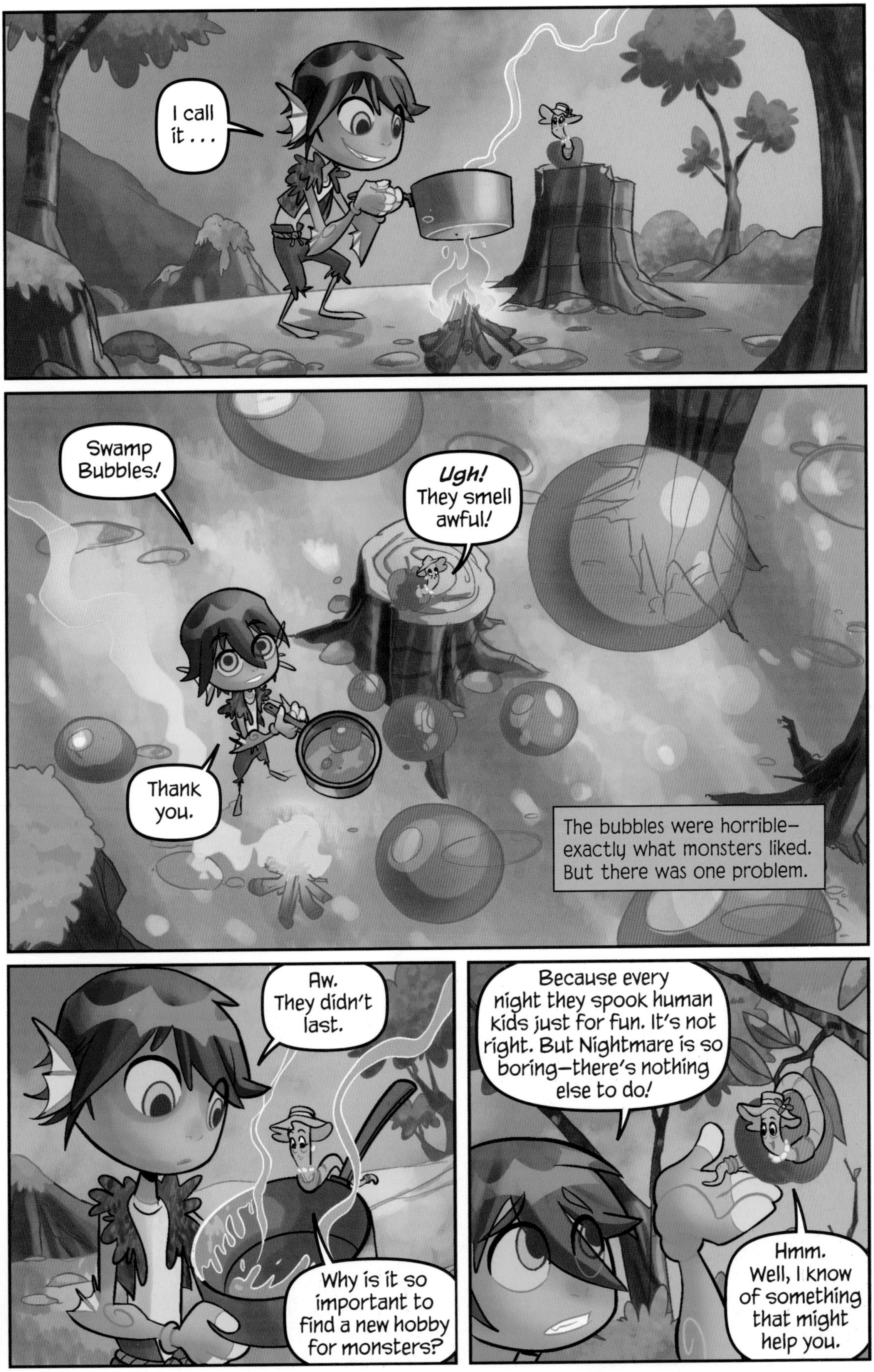
I call it . . .
Swamp Bubbles!
Ugh! They smell awful!
Thank you.
The bubbles were horrible—exactly what monsters liked. But there was one problem.
Aw. They didn't last.
Why is it so important to find a new hobby for monsters?
Because every night they spook human kids just for fun. It's not right. But Nightmare is so boring—there's nothing else to do!
Hmm. Well, I know of something that might help you.

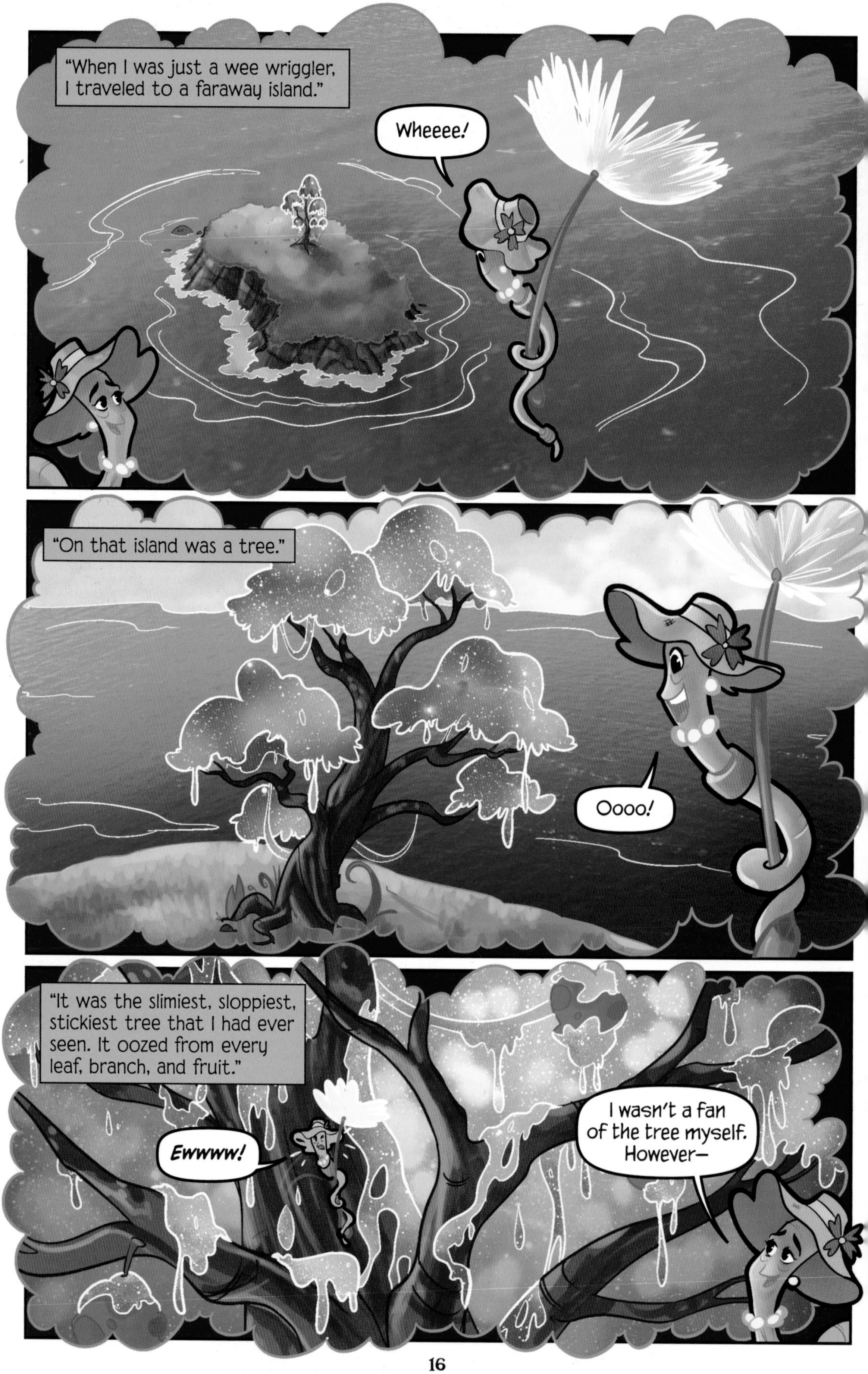
"When I was just a wee wriggler, I traveled to a faraway island."
Wheeee!
"On that island was a tree."
Oooo!
"It was the slimiest, sloppiest, stickiest tree that I had ever seen. It oozed from every leaf, branch, and fruit."
Ewwww!
I wasn't a fan of the tree myself. However—

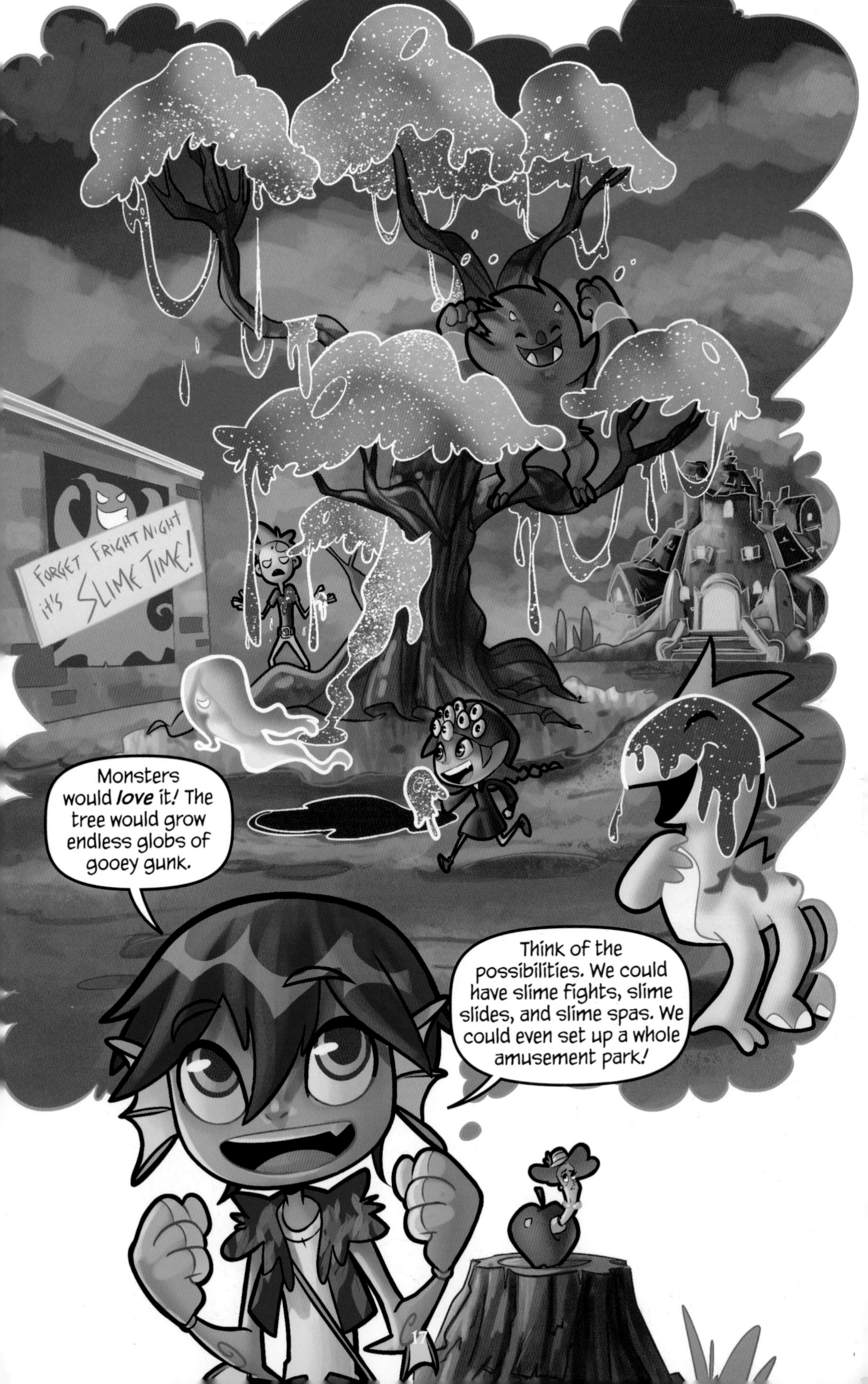
FORGET FRIGHT NIGHT it's SLIME TIME!
Monsters would *love* it! The tree would grow endless globs of gooey gunk.
Think of the possibilities. We could have slime fights, slime slides, and slime spas. We could even set up a whole amusement park!

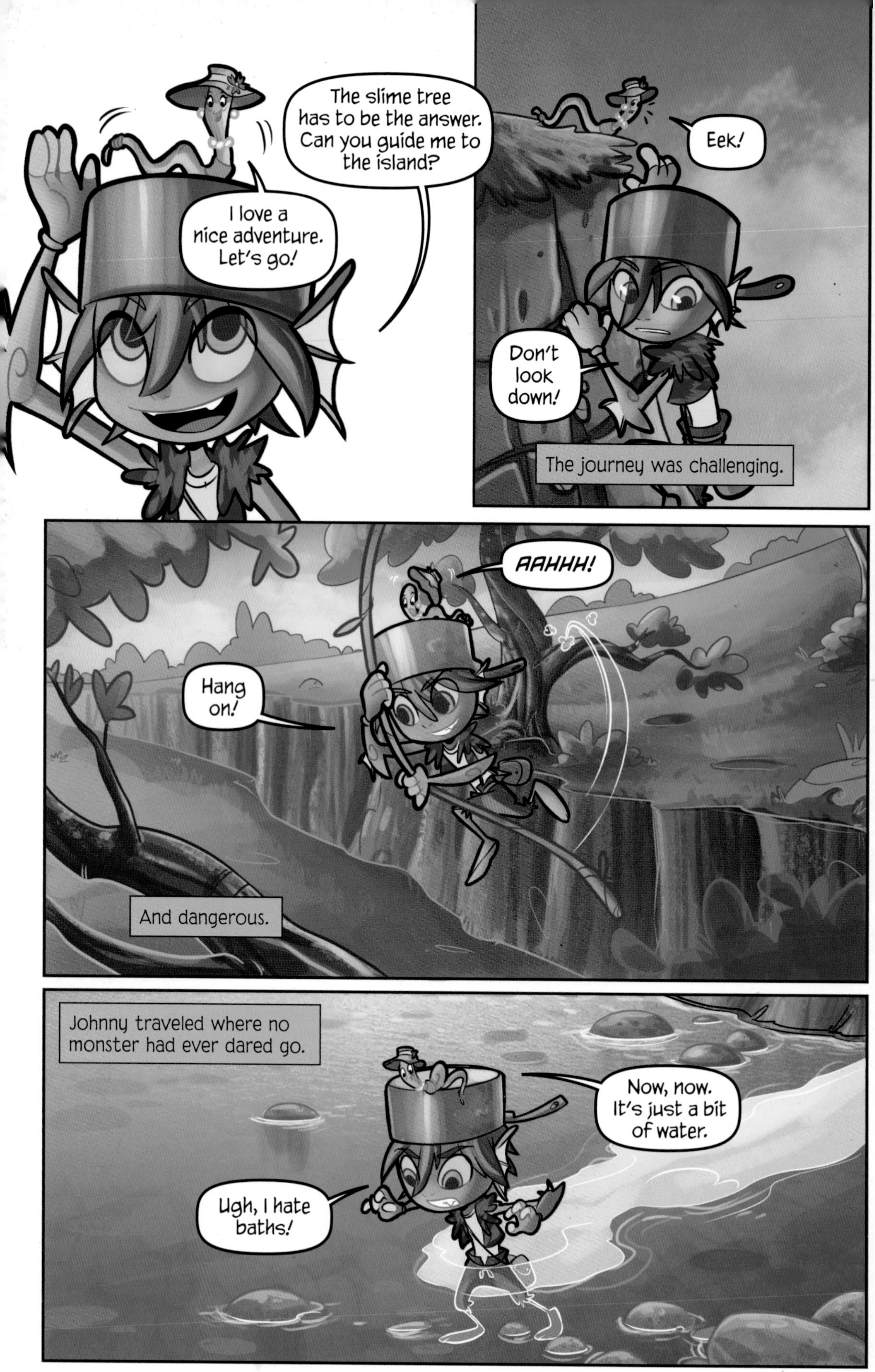
I love a nice adventure. Let's go!
The slime tree has to be the answer. Can you guide me to the island?
Eek!
Don't look down!
The journey was challenging.
AAHHH!
Hang on!
And dangerous.
Johnny traveled where no monster had ever dared go.
Now, now. It's just a bit of water.
Ugh, I hate baths!

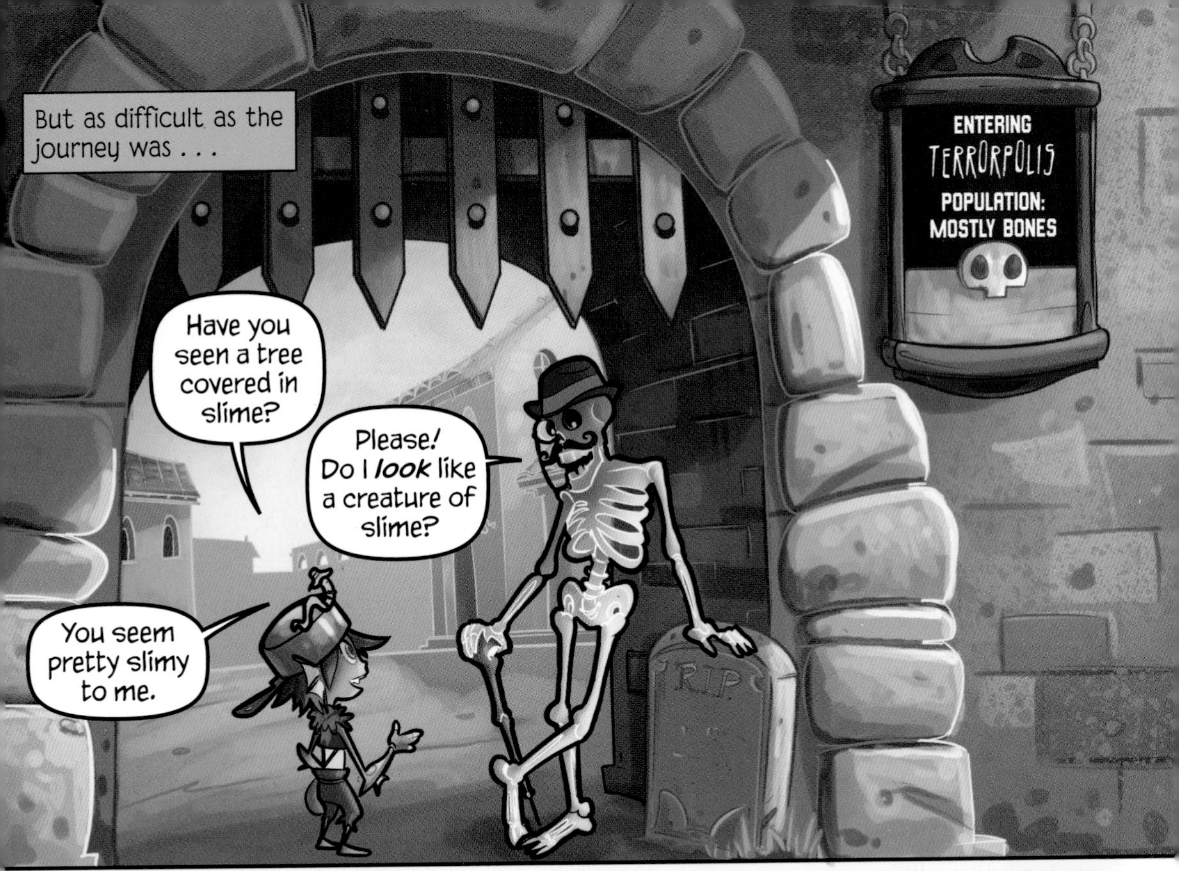
But as difficult as the journey was . . .
ENTERING TERRORPOLIS POPULATION: MOSTLY BONES
Have you seen a tree covered in slime?
Please! Do I *look* like a creature of slime?
You seem pretty slimy to me.
R.I.P.

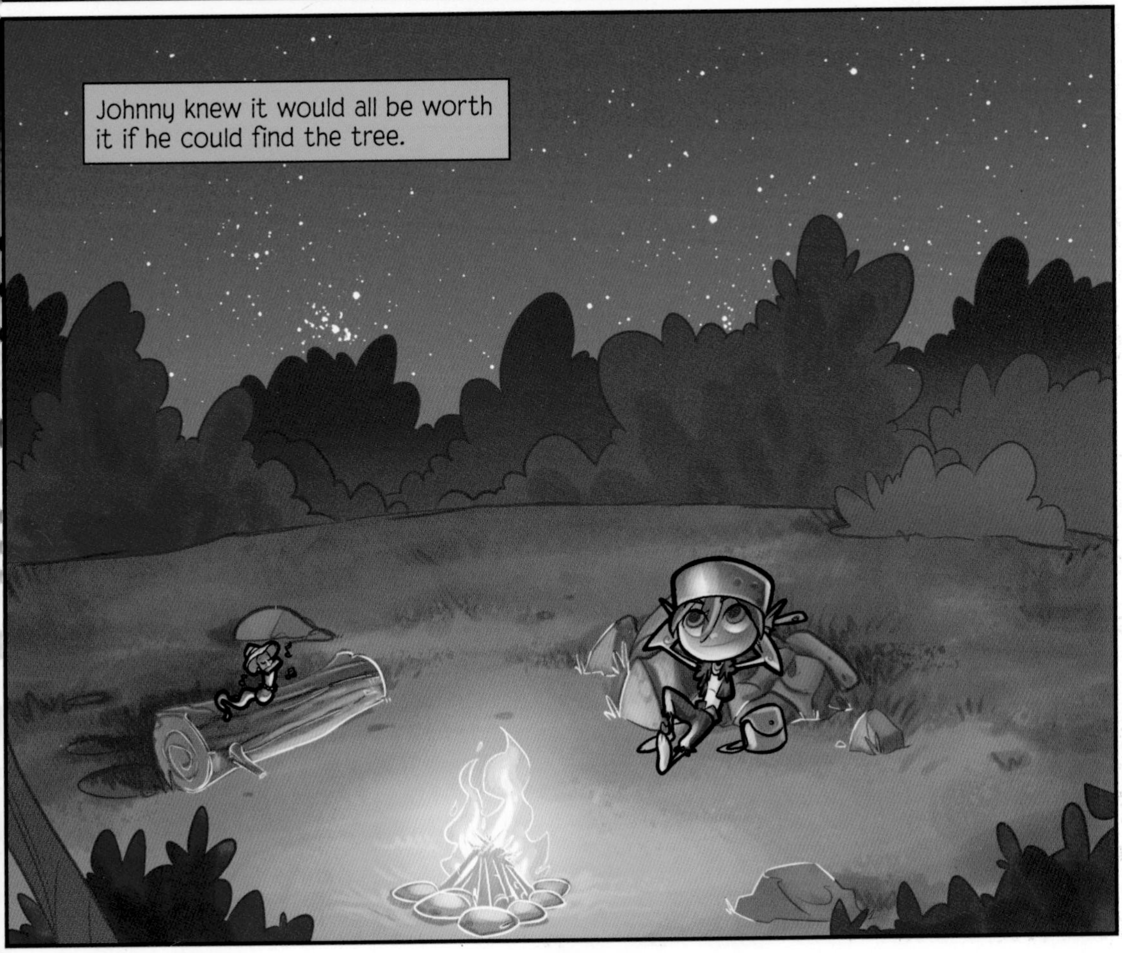
Johnny knew it would all be worth it if he could find the tree.

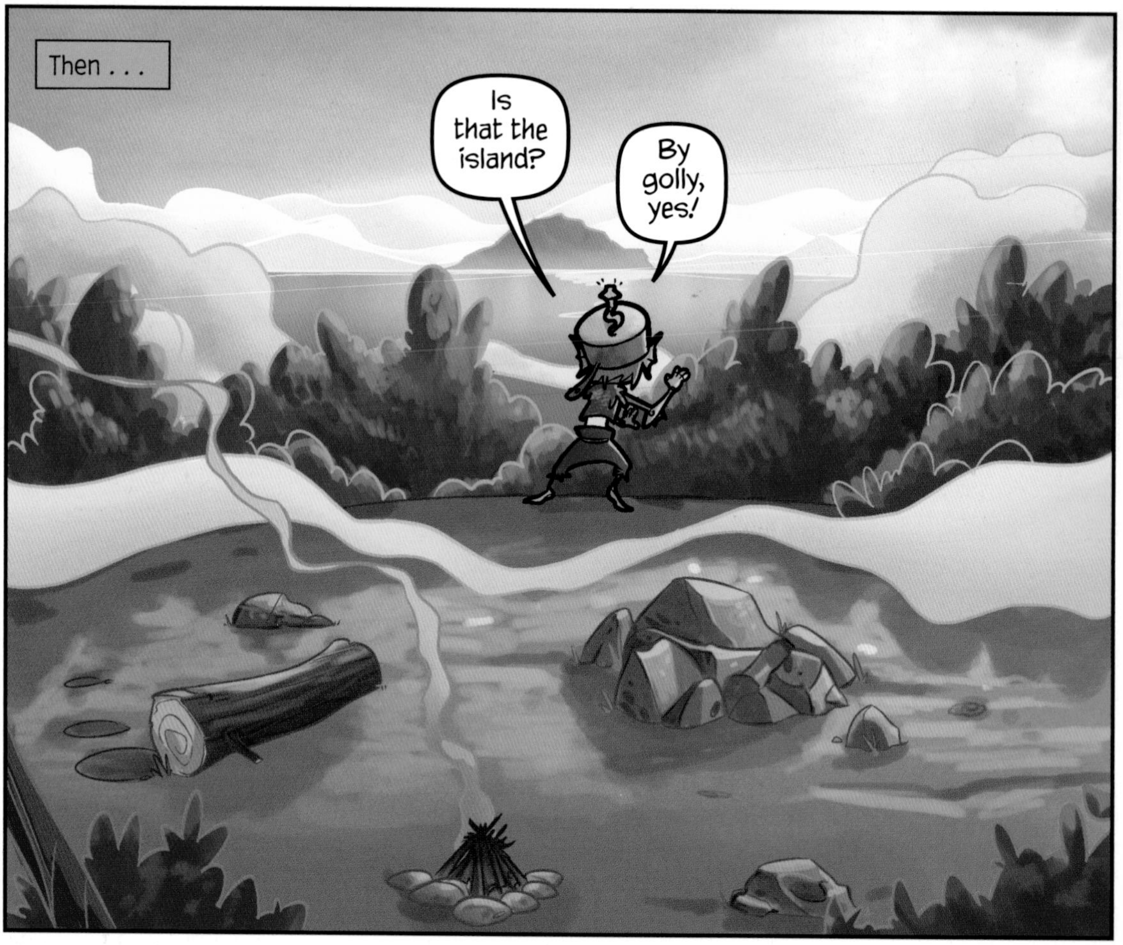
Then . . .
Is that the island?
By golly, yes!

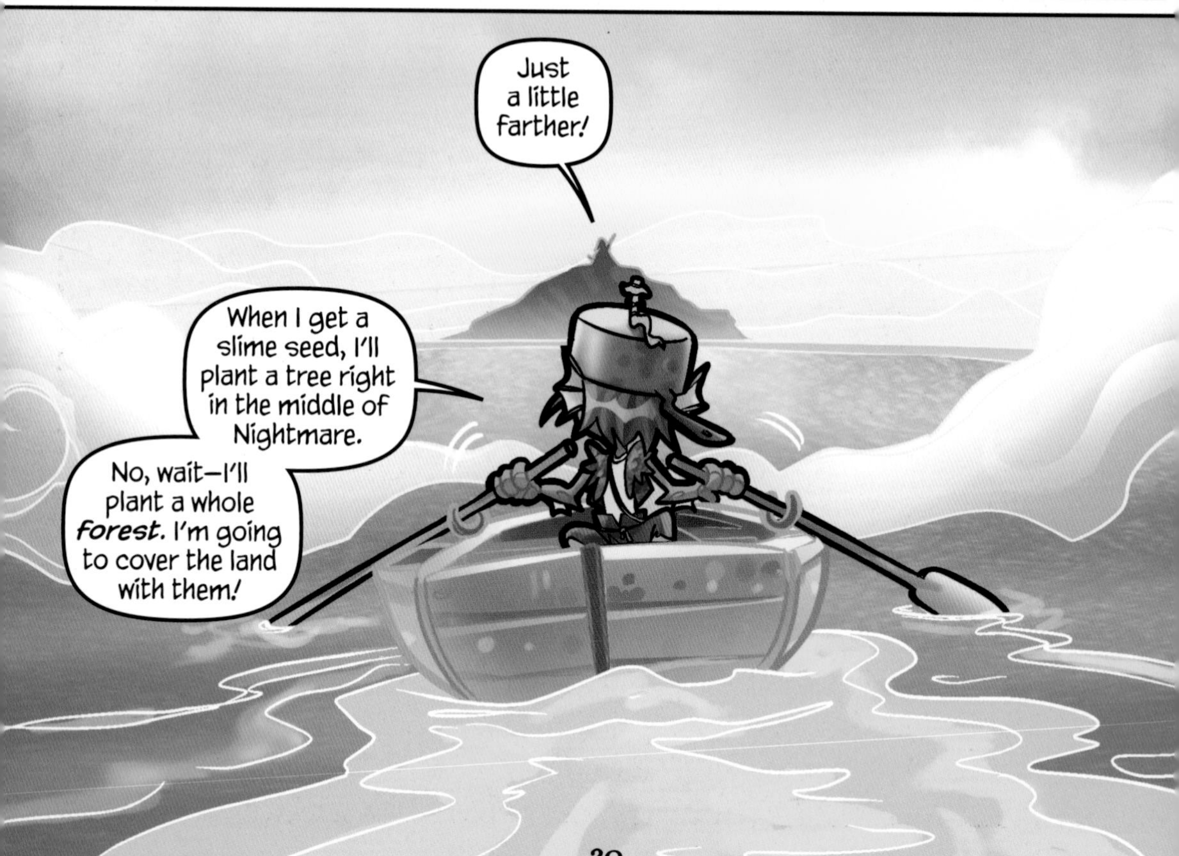
Just a little farther!
When I get a slime seed, I'll plant a tree right in the middle of Nightmare.
No, wait—I'll plant a whole *forest*. I'm going to cover the land with them!

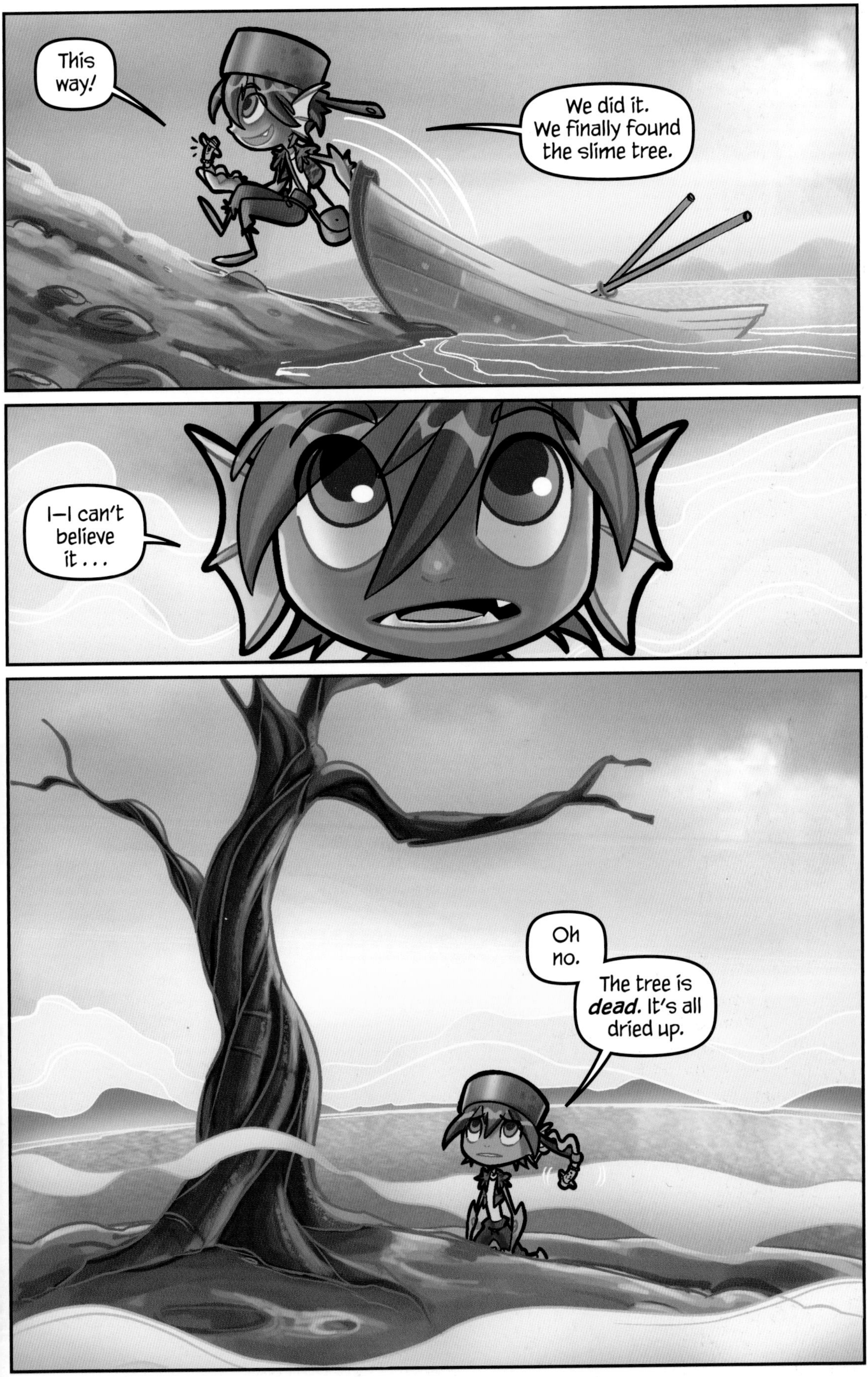
This way!
We did it. We finally found the slime tree.
I—I can't believe it . . .
Oh no.
The tree is *dead.* It's all dried up.

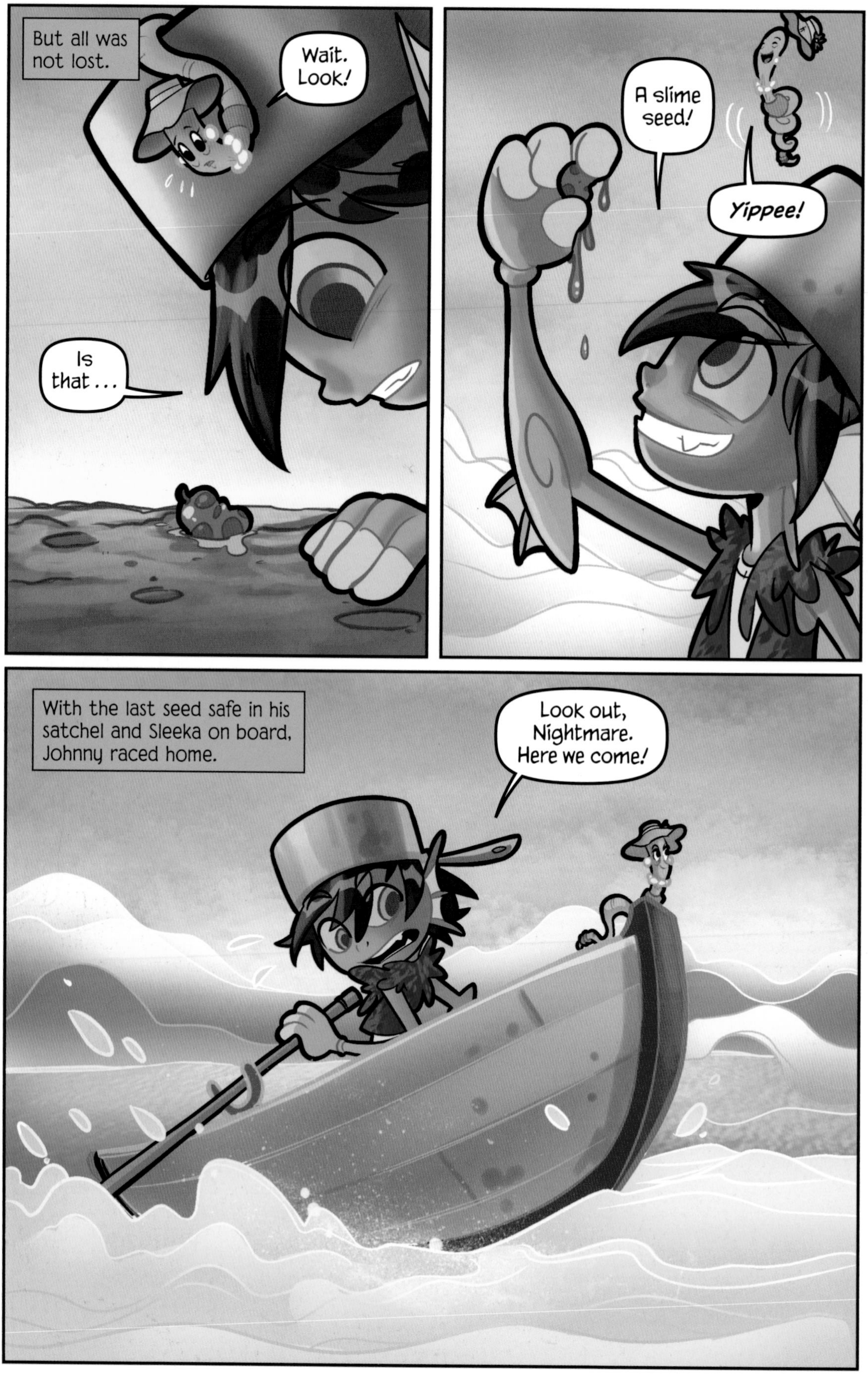

But all was not lost.
Wait. Look!
Is that . . .
A slime seed!
Yippee!
With the last seed safe in his satchel and Sleeka on board, Johnny raced home.
Look out, Nightmare. Here we come!

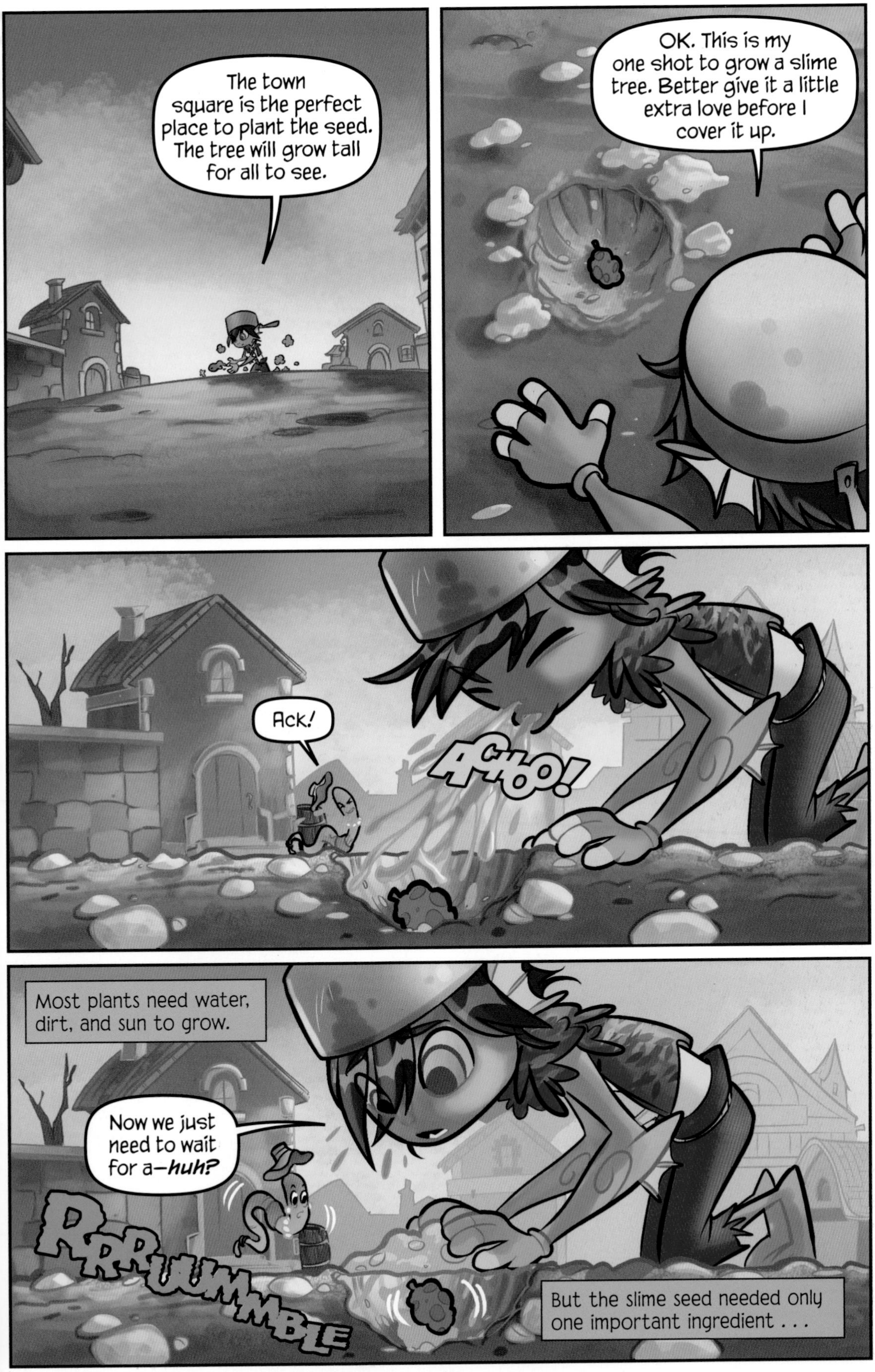
The town square is the perfect place to plant the seed. The tree will grow tall for all to see.
OK. This is my one shot to grow a slime tree. Better give it a little extra love before I cover it up.
Ack!
ACHOO!
Most plants need water, dirt, and sun to grow.
Now we just need to wait for a—*huh?*
RRRUUMMBLE
But the slime seed needed only one important ingredient . . .

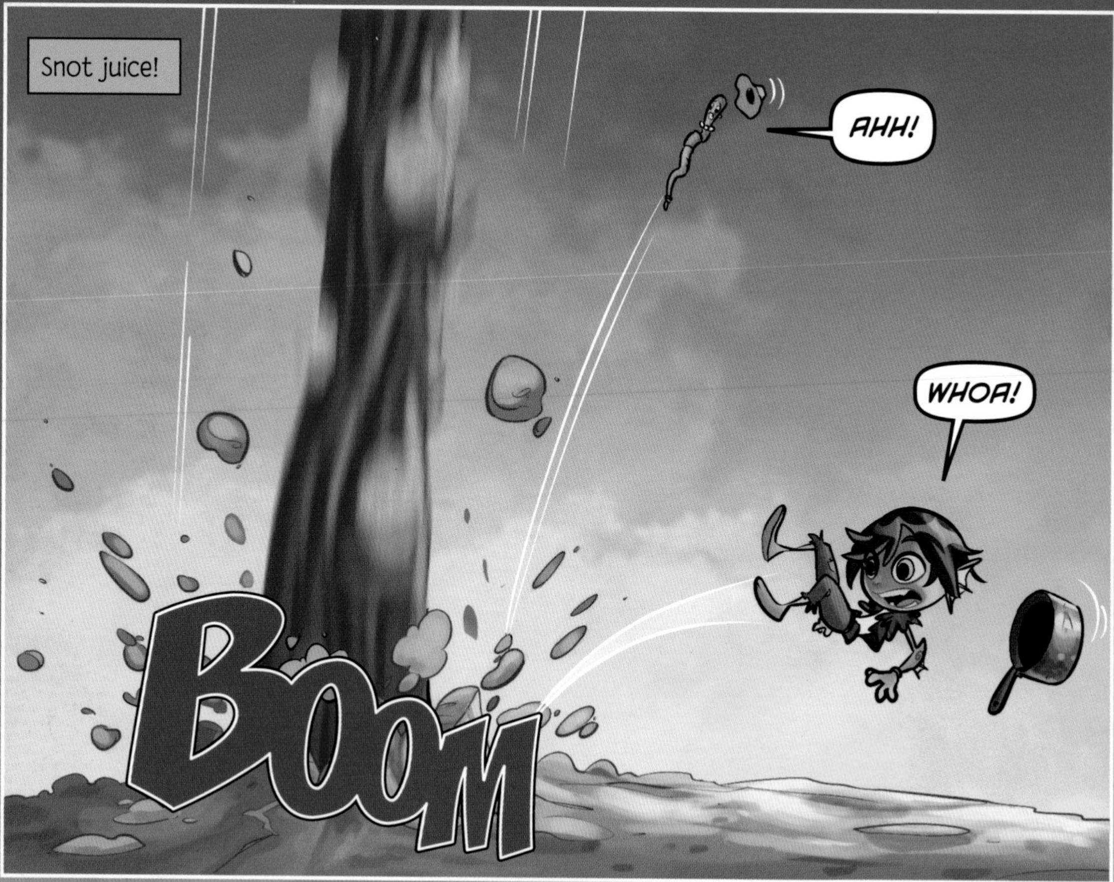
Snot juice!
AHH!
WHOA!
BOOM

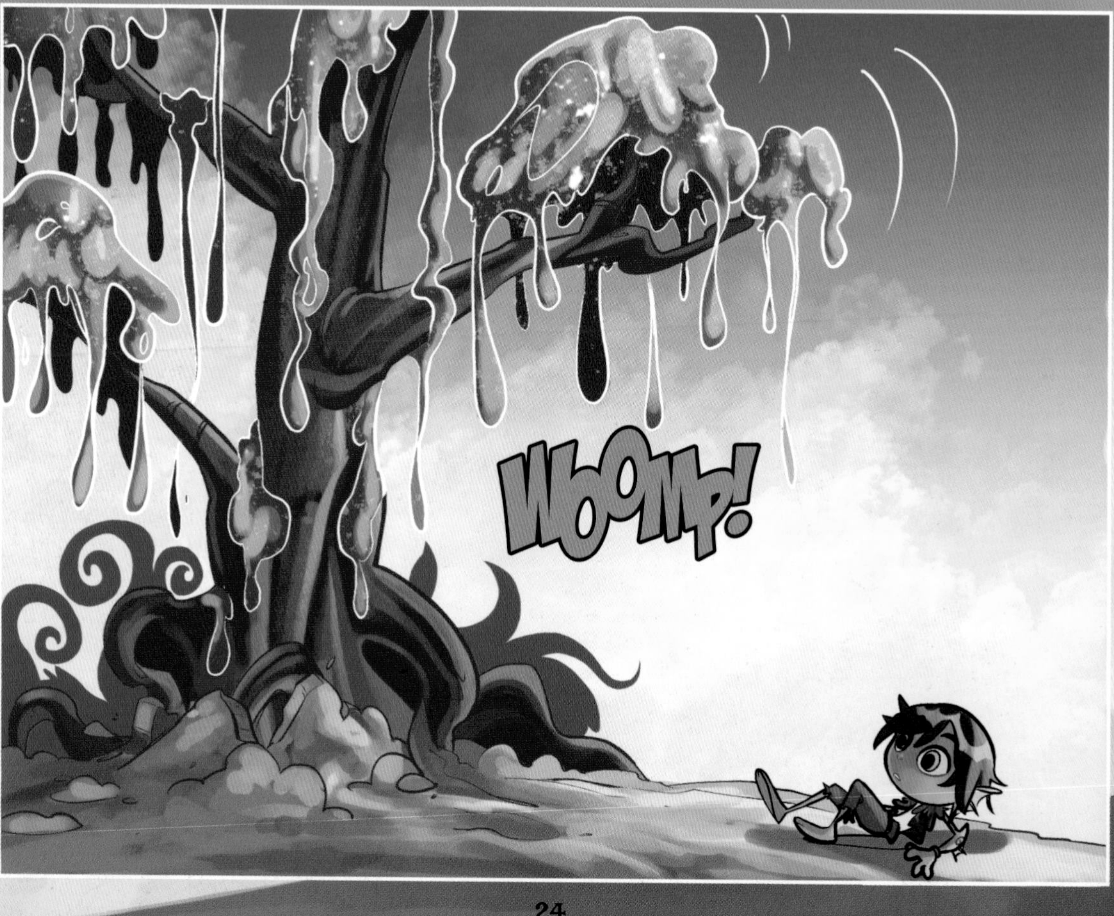
WOOMP!

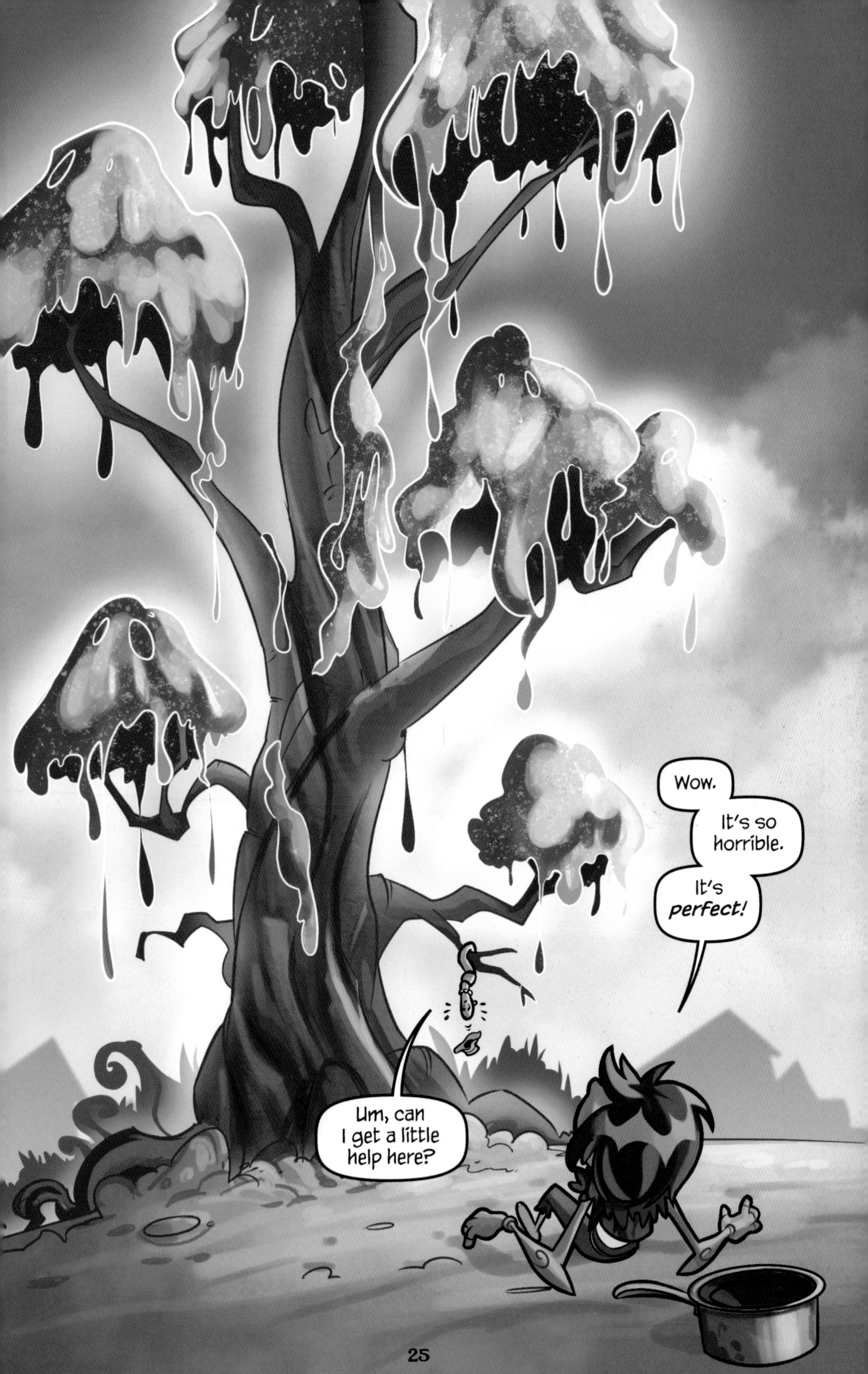
Wow.
It's so horrible.
It's *perfect!*
Um, can I get a little help here?

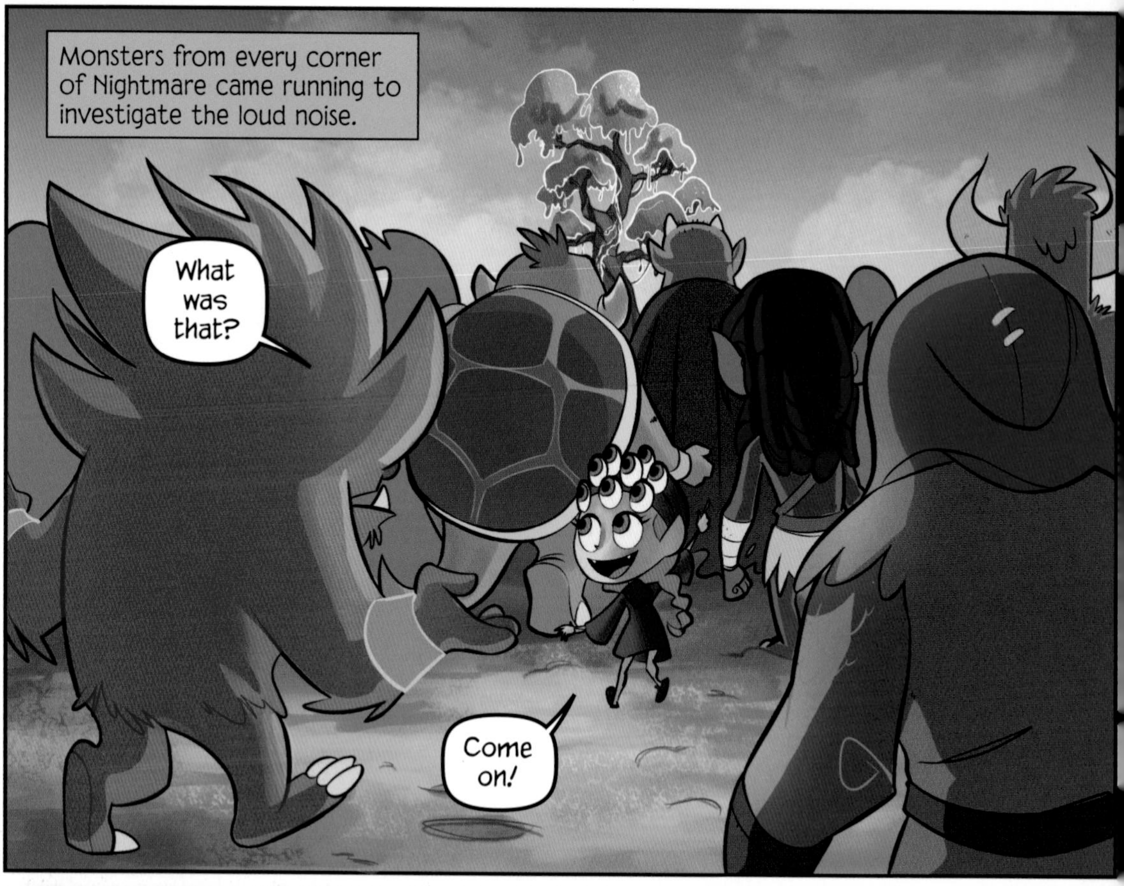
Monsters from every corner of Nightmare came running to investigate the loud noise.
What was that?
Come on!

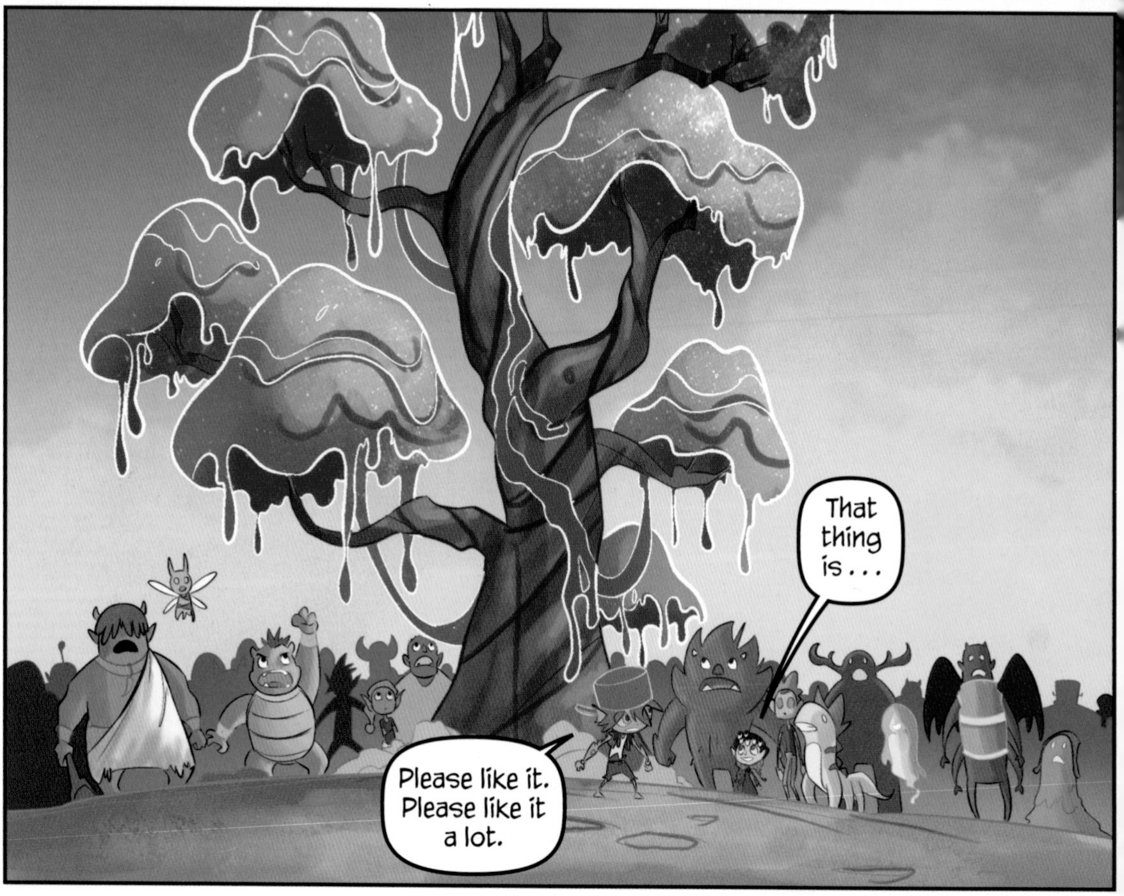
That thing is . . .
Please like it. Please like it a lot.

AMAZING!

It was everything Johnny had dreamed it would be.

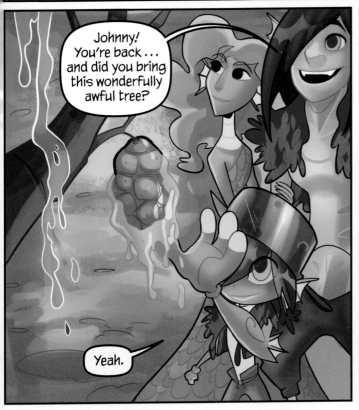

Johnny! You're back... and did you bring this wonderfully awful tree?

Yeah.

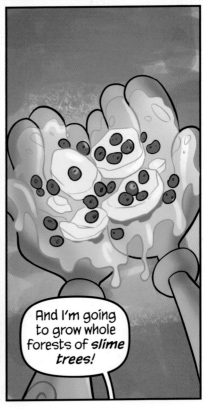

And I'm going to grow whole forests of *slime trees!*

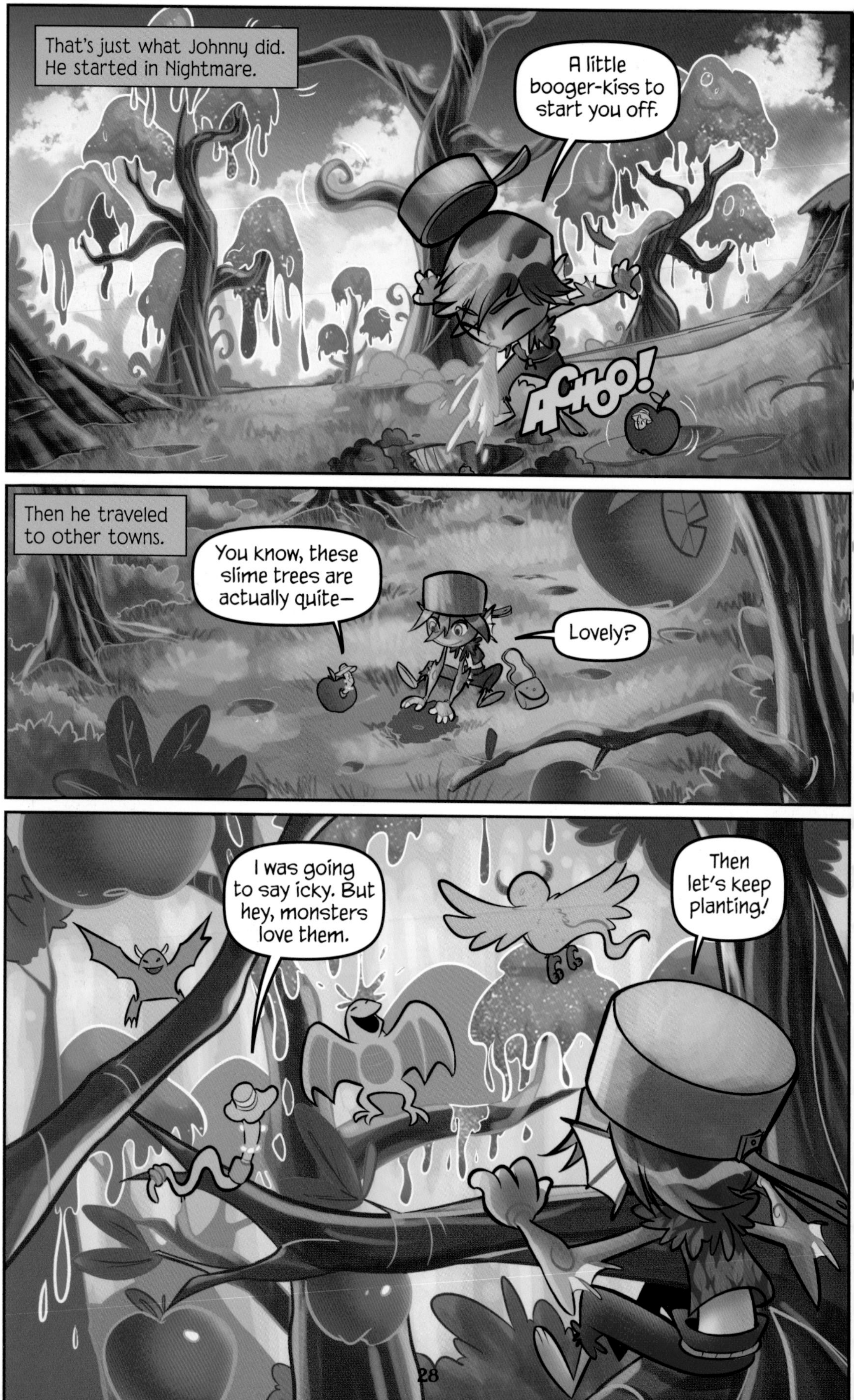
That's just what Johnny did. He started in Nightmare.
A little booger-kiss to start you off.
ACHOO!
Then he traveled to other towns.
You know, these slime trees are actually quite—
Lovely?
I was going to say icky. But hey, monsters love them.
Then let's keep planting!

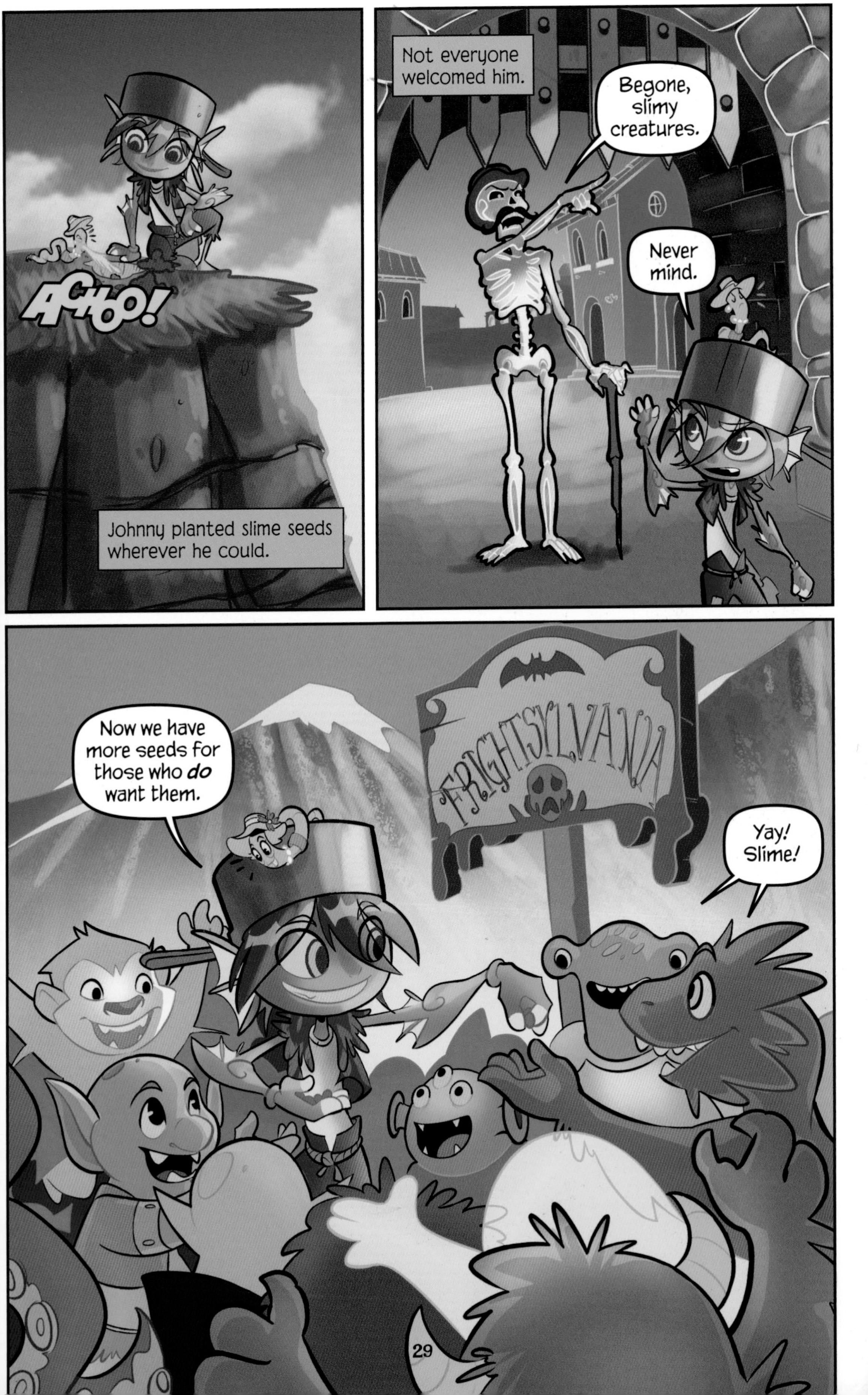
ACHOO!
Johnny planted slime seeds wherever he could.
Not everyone welcomed him.
Begone, slimy creatures.
Never mind.
Now we have more seeds for those who *do* want them.
FRIGHTSYLVANIA
Yay! Slime!

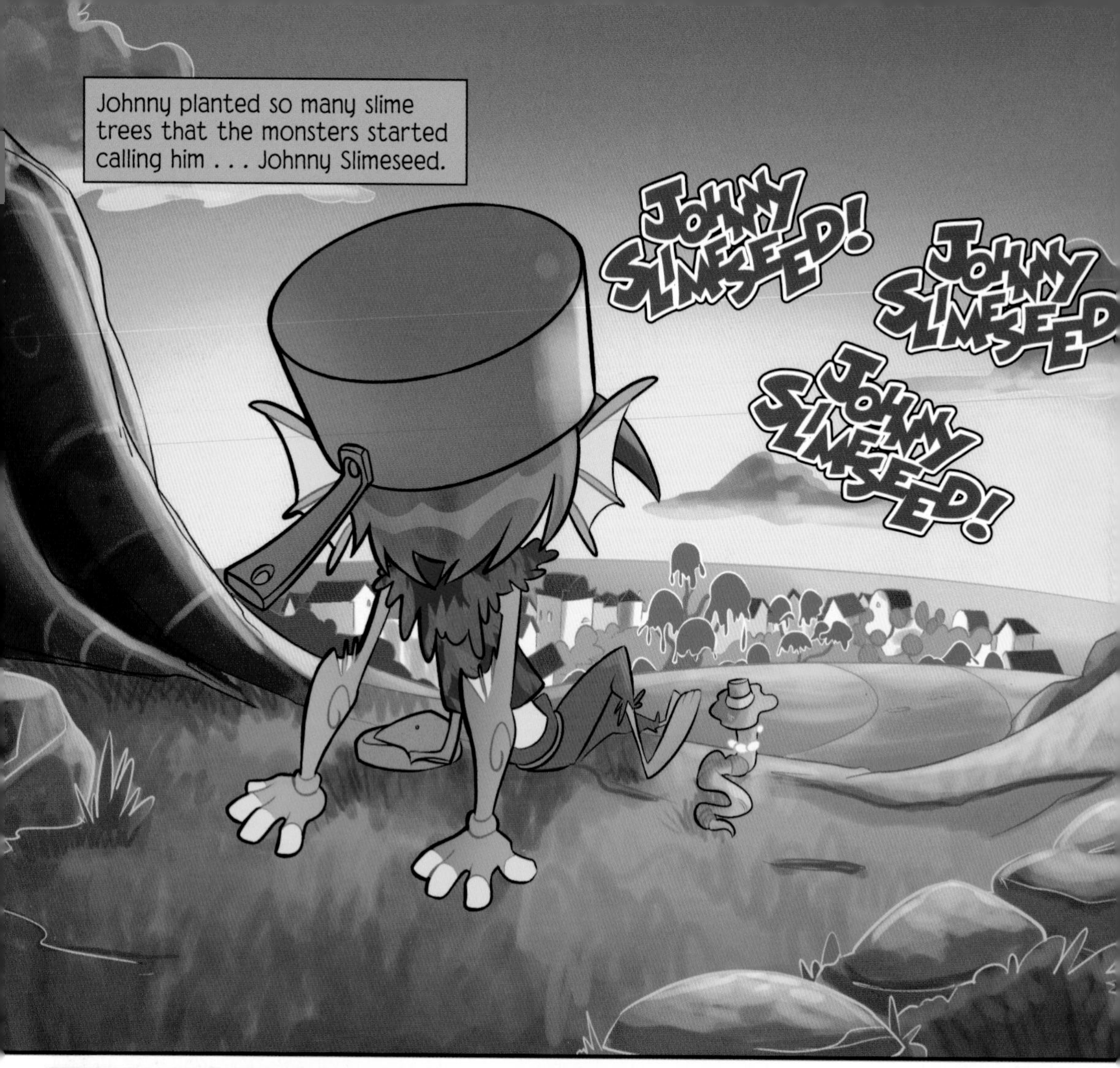
Johnny planted so many slime trees that the monsters started calling him . . . Johnny Slimeseed.
JOHNNY SLIMESEED!
JOHNNY SLIMESEED!
JOHNNY SLIMESEED!

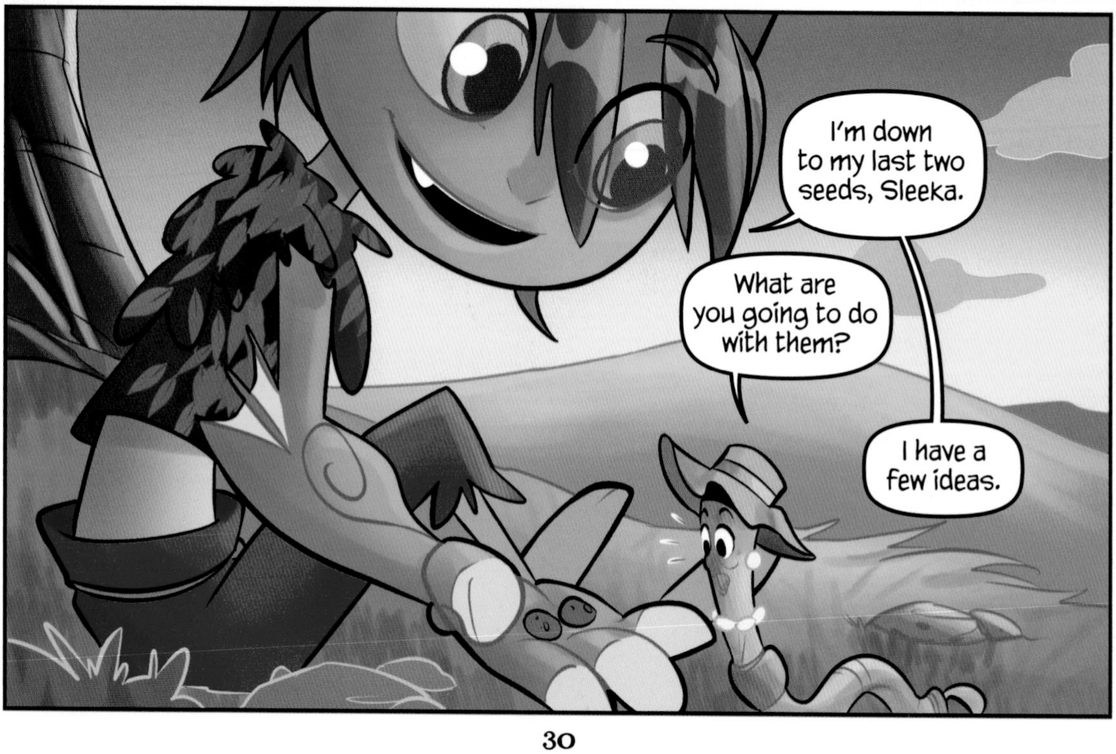
I'm down to my last two seeds, Sleeka.
What are you going to do with them?
I have a few ideas.

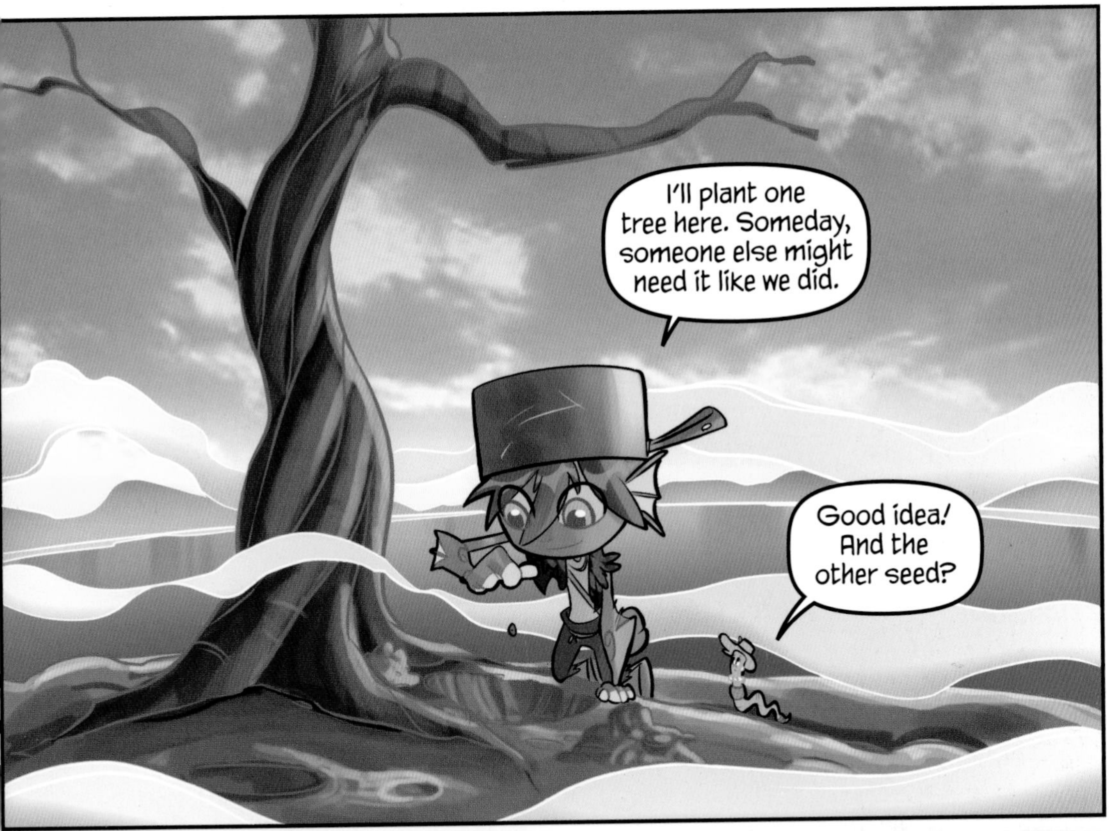
I'll plant one tree here. Someday, someone else might need it like we did.
Good idea! And the other seed?

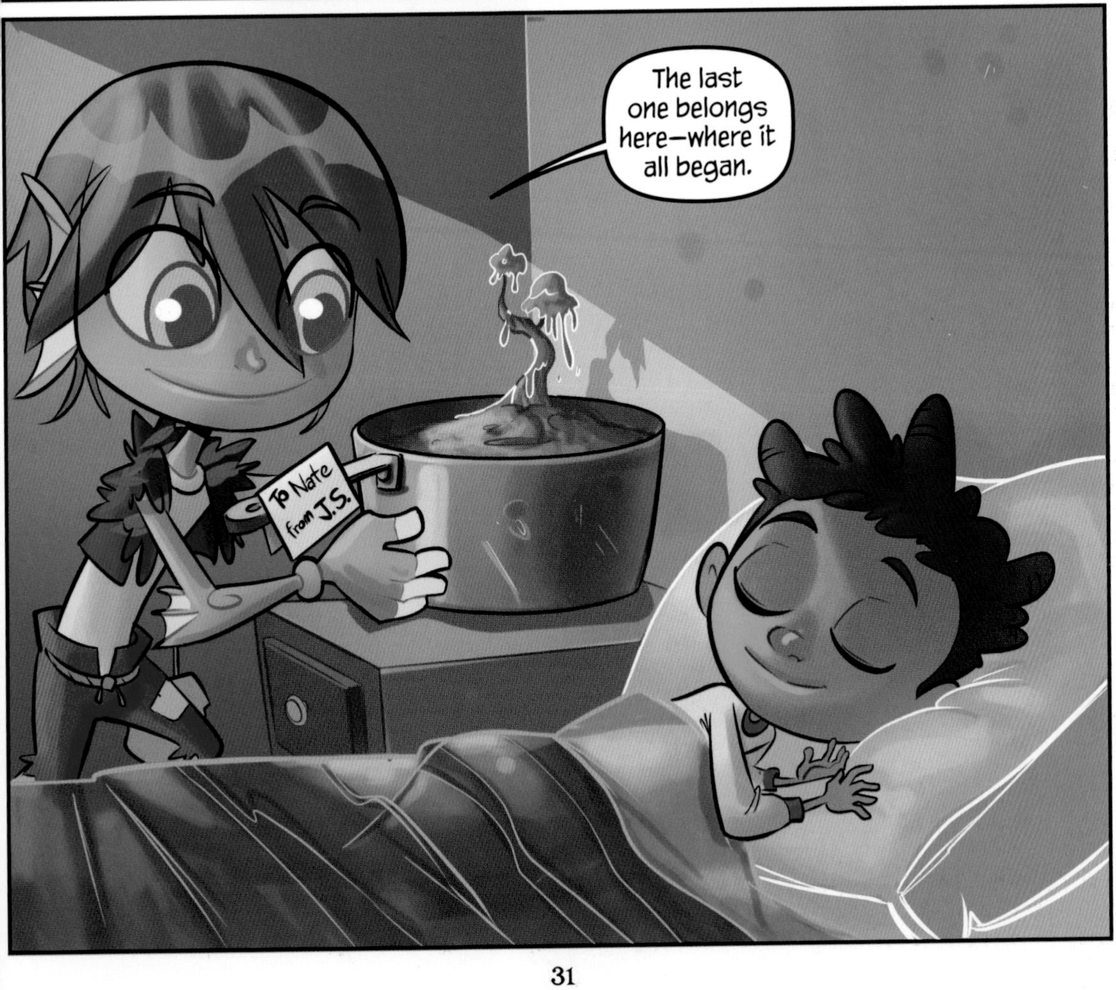
The last one belongs here—where it all began.
To Nate from J.S.

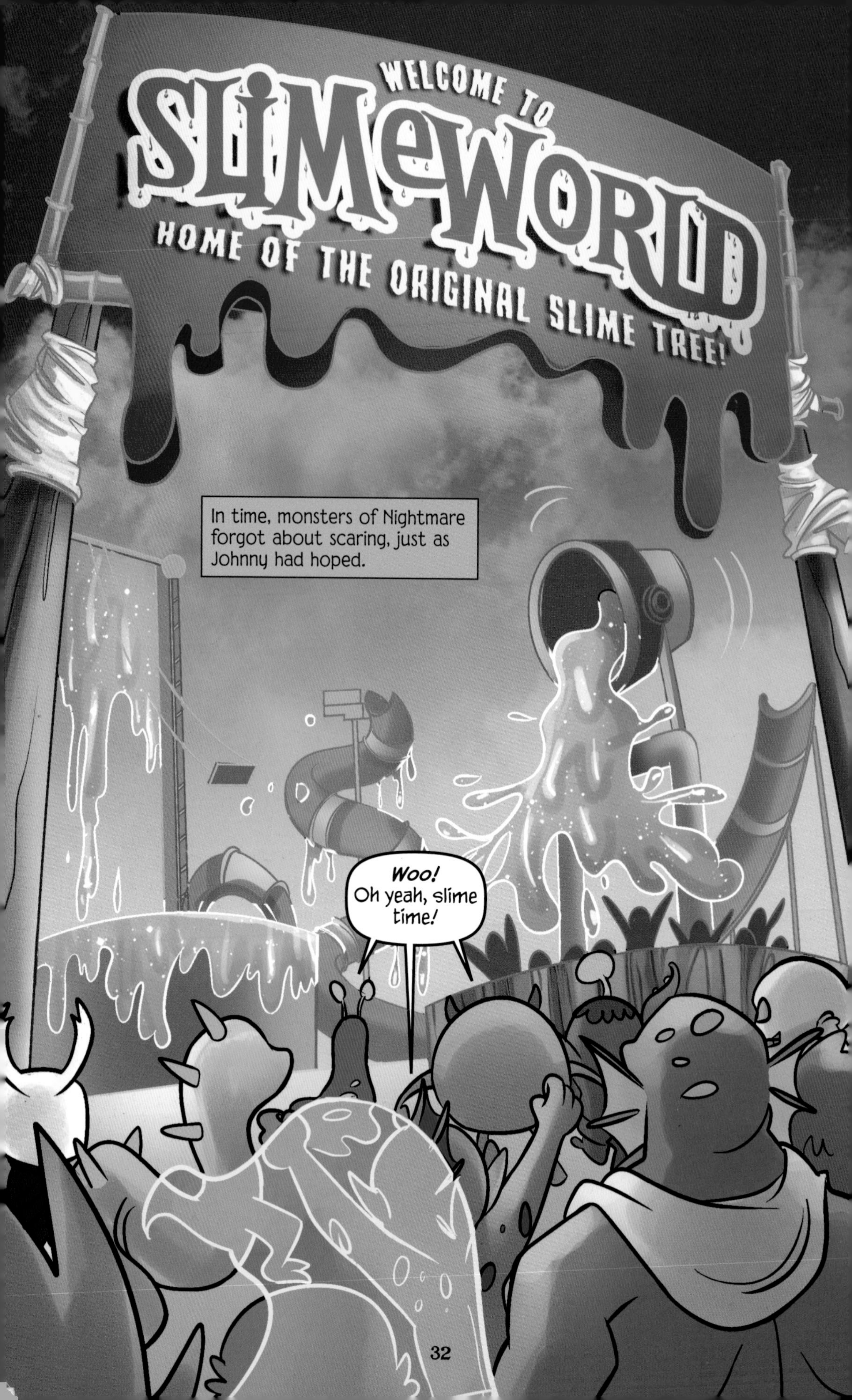
WELCOME TO
SLIMEWORLD
HOME OF THE ORIGINAL SLIME TREE!
In time, monsters of Nightmare forgot about scaring, just as Johnny had hoped.
Woo! Oh yeah, slime time!

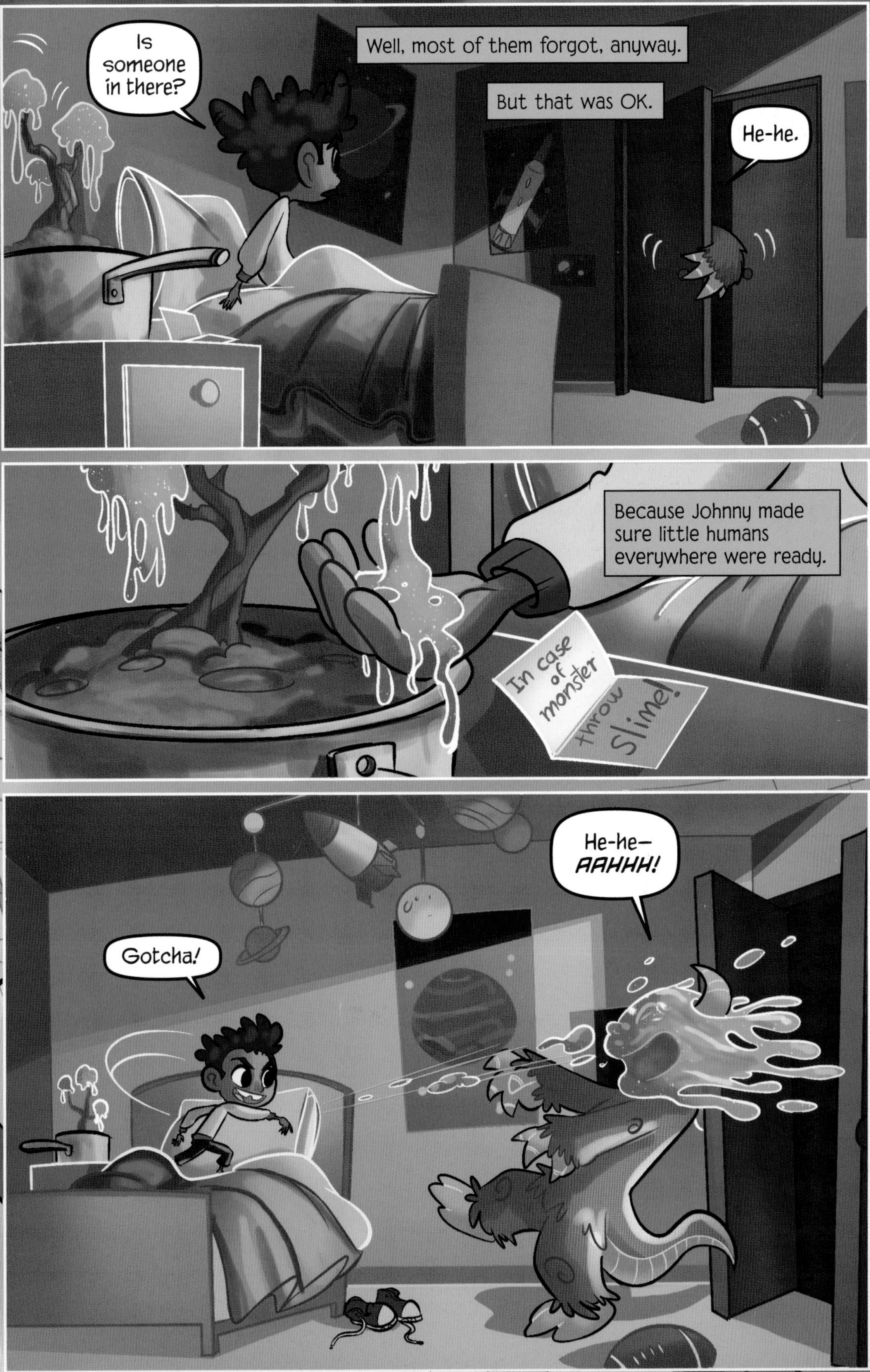
Is someone in there?
Well, most of them forgot, anyway.
But that was OK.
He-he.
Because Johnny made sure little humans everywhere were ready.
In case of monster
throw slime!
He-he—AAHHH!
Gotcha!

ALL ABOUT THE ORIGINAL TALE!

A folktale is a story that's told over and over again and passed down through generations. The story of a wandering gardener named Johnny Appleseed is actually based on a real person named John Chapman.

John was born in Massachusetts on September 26, 1774. His father fought in the Revolutionary War. His mother died when he was young. John's father remarried and had a total of ten children. When he was eighteen, John left his overcrowded home. For the next fifty years, he traveled throughout the wildernesses of Pennsylvania, Ohio, and Indiana. Along the way, he planted apple seeds. Later, pioneers were able to purchase the young trees and plant their own orchards. The apples weren't very good for eating, but they could be made into valuable cider.

John was known for his odd appearance. He used an old coffee sack for a shirt, and he often wouldn't wear any shoes. Some say John even wore a tin pan as a hat over his long hair.

In stories, Johnny Appleseed loved all living creatures. One tale tells of how he saved an injured wolf pup that then stayed with him throughout his travels. Another says he was brokenhearted over killing a snake that tried (and failed) to sink its fangs into his tough-skinned foot. A third claims he even put out a campfire when he saw mosquitoes being burned in the flames.

John kept planting until he passed away in 1845. But tales of his journeys continued to spread. In 1871, an article was published that called him Johnny Appleseed, and the legend became popular around the country.

A FAR OUT GUIDE TO THE TALE'S MONSTER TWISTS!

Johnny Appleseed is a human. But in this far out version, Johnny Slimeseed is a swamp monster!

Apple seeds have been swapped out for slime seeds that grow into disgusting goo-oozing trees!

Johnny Appleseed wants to help pioneers, but Johnny Slimeseed wants to stop other monsters from scaring kids!

The original Johnny collected his seeds from cider presses. In this tale, he has to go on an adventure to find one!

VISUAL QUESTIONS

In your own words, summarize how Johnny feels about Fright Night. (Turn back to pages 7-9 if you need help.) What in the art and text makes you think that?

In the original tale, Johnny Appleseed is known for being very gentle and kind. Do you think Johnny Slimeseed also shares this feature? Why or why not? Be sure to use examples from the story to support your answer.

You can get a lot of information just by looking at the art in graphic novels. What details do you notice in Johnny's classroom and around the town of Nightmare? What do they tell you about his world?

Why is there a dialogue bubble coming from the apple? Who's speaking? How do you know?

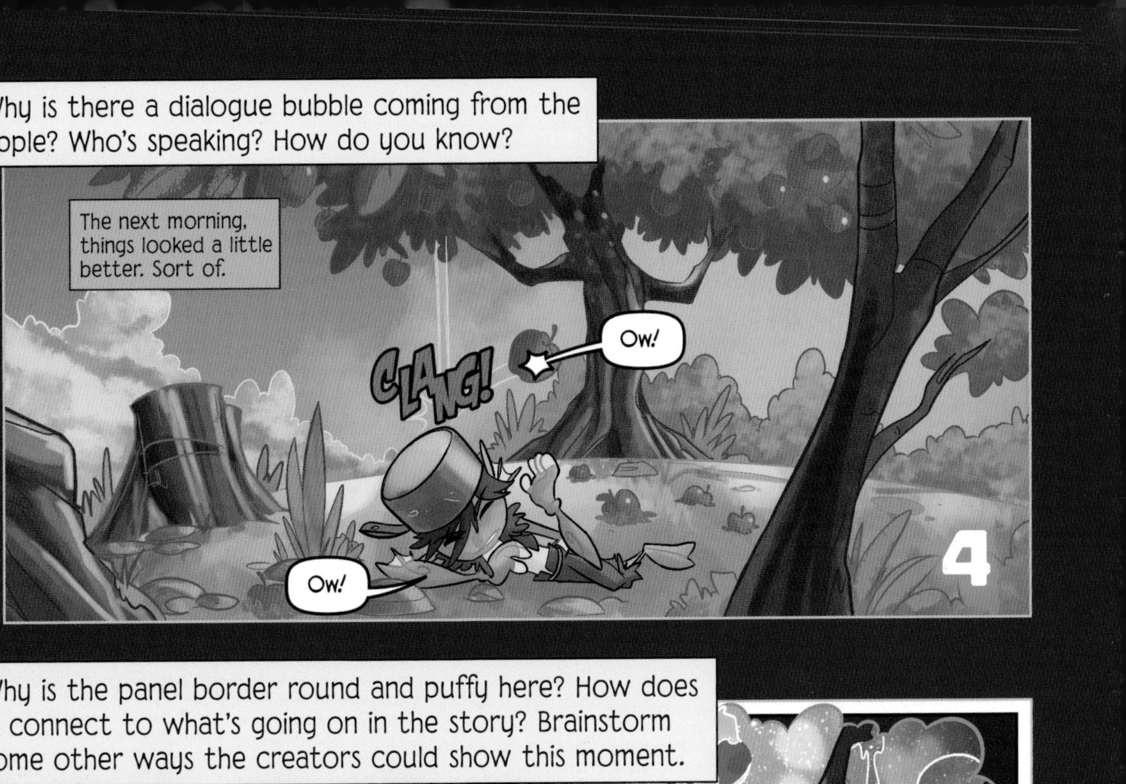
The next morning, things looked a little better. Sort of.
CLANG!
Ow!
Ow!
4

Why is the panel border round and puffy here? How does it connect to what's going on in the story? Brainstorm some other ways the creators could show this moment.

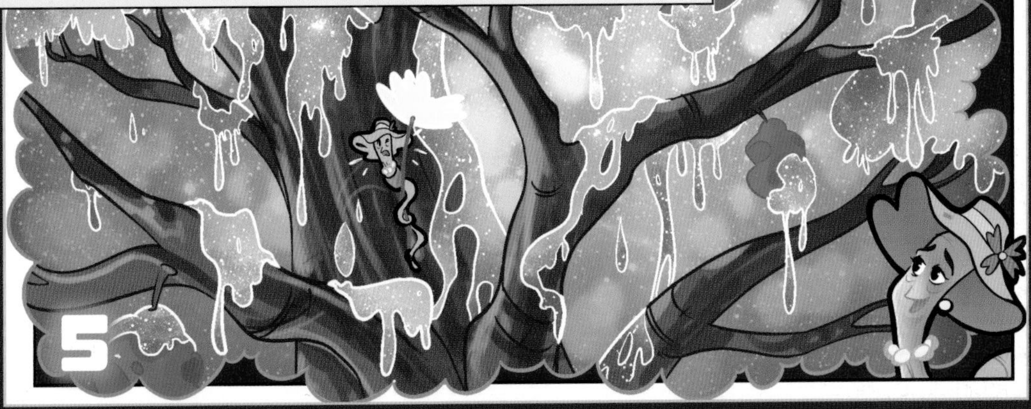
5

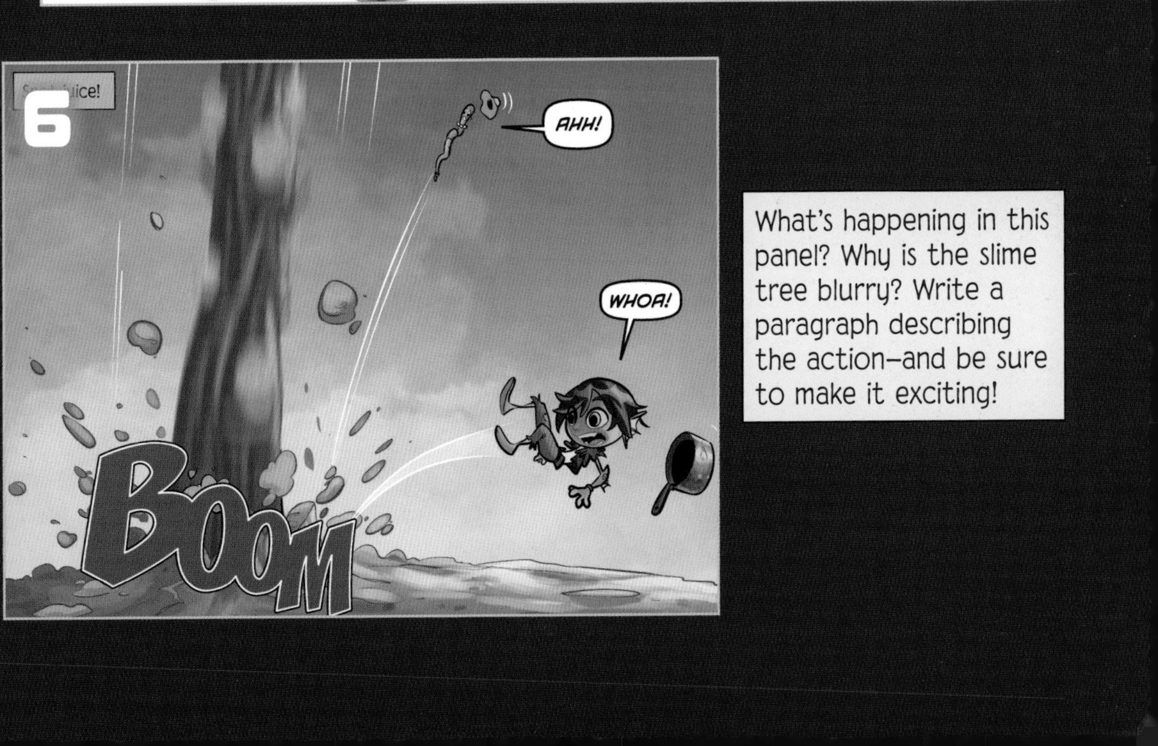
6
AHH!
WHOA!
BOOM

What's happening in this panel? Why is the slime tree blurry? Write a paragraph describing the action—and be sure to make it exciting!

AUTHOR

Stephanie True Peters worked as a children's book editor for ten years before she started writing books herself. She has since written forty books, including *Sleeping Beauty*, *Magic Master* and the New York Times best seller *A Princess Primer: A Fairy Godmother's Guide to Being a Princess*. When not at her computer, Peters enjoys playing with her two children, hitting the gym, or working on home improvement projects with her patient and supportive husband, Daniel.

ILLUSTRATOR

Berenice Muñiz is a graphic designer and illustrator from Monterrey, Mexico. In the past, she has done work for publicity agencies, art exhibitions, and she's even created her own webcomic. These days, Berenice is devoted to illustrating comics as part of the Graphikslava crew. In her spare time, "Bere" loves to draw, read manga, watch animated movies, play video games, and fight zombies.